Lock Down Publications
and Ca$h Presents

The Black Diamond Cartel 2

By SayNoMore

Lock Down Publications
P.O. Box 944
Stockbridge, GA 30281
www.lockdownpublications.com

Like our page on Facebook: Lock Down Publications
www.facebook.com/lockdownpublications.ldp

Stay Connected with Us!

PROLOGUE

Blanka looked at the girl standing in front of him. He took his finger and placed it under her chin, lifted her head up and looked into her eyes. He then looked at Hector.

"How old is she?" He removed his finger from her chin.

"Sixteen-seventeen at the most."

"What is her name?"

"Selina."

Blanka looked at her one more time before turning his attention back to Hector.

"Clean her up, she's fresh, three hundred dollars to break her in. Start off with just three men a night."

Blanka's conversation was interrupted when his maid walked up to him.

"Mr. Blanka, your guest has arrived."

"Good, escort him to the back deck. I will be there shortly."

"Yes sir."

"I have to go take care of something. Do as I said with her, and I will see you later." Blanka patted Hector on the back and strode off to his house.

He walked through the living room to the backyard deck. Malachi looked at him as he walked through the doors right up to him, prompting Malachi to stand up.

"Malachi, it's good to meet you. Please have a seat." Blanka extended his hand to shake Malachi's hand.

Malachi looked at the tall Hispanic man wearing a white and pink suit with white shoes. As they sat down, Blanka reached in his top jacket pocket and pulled out two Cuban cigars, passing one to Malachi.

"Thank you for the cigar, Blanka."

4

"No problem. So, tell me what can I do for you, Malachi? I took this meeting out of respect for Red-Invee. She speaks very highly of you."

Malachi lowered his head and lit his cigar.

"New York City is full of corruption, extortion, and murder, but more importantly, money. I want it *all*."

Blanka looked at the dark-skinned man in front of him, sitting on his deck. Blanka smiled and pulled on his cigar.

"What about the men who have the same dream as you, Malachi? You going to kill them all?"

"Blanka, name one king who hasn't caught a few bodies on the way to ascending his throne? These are the rules to the streets we live by. At anytime, someone can be killed or kidnapped. These are the rules. This is the game we play."

"I heard stories about you, Malachi, and your ruthlessness."

Blanka stopped talking when his maid came outside with a bucket of ice, two wine glasses, and a bottle of champagne. She placed everything down on the table next to a magazine that was faced down before walking off. Malachi looked at the lady as she was leaving the deck.

"I like you, Malachi. I can see in your eyes you are focused and driven. I don't smell the cloying scent of weakness on you, but there is only one problem we might have that will stop us from the success of accomplishing what we can have together."

Malachi pulled on his cigar.

"What is that, Blanka?"

Blanka reached on the table and turned over the GQ magazine with Malachi on the cover. The title read, *The New King of New York City*.

"You see Malachi, acting too flashy can be bad for business. If we do this, we play by *my* rules, not yours. The first rule is this can never happen again."

"So, in so many words, I will be under the cartel bander?"

"I only deal with the cartel, no one on the outside. So that should answer your question."

"Will I run my own cartel?"

"You will run your own cartel in New York, but *you* will answer to *me*, and Malachi, being in the cartel, you can't have a heart. You will be a part of human trafficking, drug trades, and extortion, along with prostitution of all ages, you will Gorilla breed when I tell you to. This is a new level of the game you are stepping into. You will walk the path of life or death. Either way, I'ma walk you down one of them."

Malachi walked up to Blanka, "I run my cartel and answer to you, no one else?"

"Yes, to both of your questions."

Malachi put his hand out and shook Blanka's hand.

"Good... let 's go have a drink and come take a walk with me. There's something I want to show you."

Blanka poured both of them a drink, then walked Malachi to the far end of the property to a workshop he had constructed a couple months back. When Blanka opened the door there was one man there. Malachi looked at him then at the burning hot flame with an iron rod with a symbol of two guns crossing each other and a pitchfork going down the middle of them.

"Malachi, if you don't mind, lift your right shirtsleeve up for Hector, please."

Malachi pulled his shirt sleeve up and walked over to Hector who was standing next to the burning hot flames. Then he looked at Blanka.

"Blanka, you come and do it. This is your stamp. You give it to me."

Blanka nodded.

"I will do it, Hector."

Blanka pulled the rod out the flames and walked up to Malachi.

"Flesh of my flesh, blood of my blood, loyalty to my brother, death to disloyalty. Malachi, this is going to hurt. Endure the pain, my brother."

Blanka placed the burning hot symbol on Malachi's arm and pressed down. Malachi bit down on his teeth and looked Blanka in the eyes as sweat came down his face. Blanka pulled the rod off his arm and smiled and nodded at Malachi as he shook his hand.

"Good… now come. We have much business to discuss, Brother."

Chapter 1

Four years later

"New York City needs to wake up and face the facts, we have the cartel in our city now, and there's no denying it. Look at the events that have taken place over the last year to the recent one just a few weeks ago."

Captain Fuller sat quietly across from Stacy Hall from WAKE UP NEW YORK was talking.

"Mrs. Hall, there is no proof that the cartel is in New York City. These are baseless rumors and a rumor without proof is just an empty claim, but we are investigating every incident. We are not leaving one rock unturned."

"Captain Fuller, you say it's just rumors, but not even a month ago, 15 teen females were found dead in a dirty box truck, and they all were chained to the wall on the inside of the truck. This is just one example of human and sex trafficking. We have more people dying. They are overdosing on X pills and heroin, and to add the icing on the cake, five out of the 15 teen females were reported missing. So, not only were they kidnapped but they were being forced to have sex, an inside source told us. Let's be truthful with ourselves, Captain Fuller. The cartel made its way from Mexico to El Paso, Texas, throughout California; now, they are in New York City. What is it going to take for y'all to see that they are here? A body being hung upside down from Brooklyn Bridge, cut open with a note around its neck that says, 'we are here'?"

Malachi smoked his cigar as he watched Stacy Hall from *WAKE UP NEW YORK* talk with the illustrious captain from the 25th Precinct of the New York Police Department.

When his phone went off, he put the tv on mute and answered the phone.

"Hello."

"Good morning, Malachi. I was calling to see if you are watching WAKE UP NEW YORK with Stacy Hall?"

Malachi pulled his cigar as Blanka was talking.

"I'm watching it a*s we speak.*" Blanka sat in his living room with an all-white suit on drinking a cup of coffee with his legs crossed, as he watched the scathing expose.

"So there no point to talk about what need to be done?"

"No, there isn't."

"Good, I'll be in touch." Malachi hung up the phone, leaned back in his chair, and continued to watch the interview as he formulated a plan.

***

Captain Fuller walked out the tv station, but he turned around when someone called his name. He looked and seen it was District Attorney Cox. He stopped and waited for him to catch up with him.

"Hey, just saw you on *WAKE UP NEW YORK.*"

"Yeah, that conversation went all wrong from the start, from the time I sat down."

"You know Stacy is a bulldog and she going to make a lie into the truth, and the truth into a lie."

"Yeah, but the cold fact remains that she's right. We still have Calvin Reeves and Robert Pacino, and a handful of other Mafia bosses running around pushing drugs and opening illegal gambling spots. The only thing out of this last year that works in our favor is that Malachi Williams just disappeared. That's one less fucking headache that I have to deal with. Maybe his body is just waiting to be found or it might be tied down to some bricks at the bottom of the East River. The fuck if I know."

Captain Fuller pulled out a cigarette and lit it.

"Fuller, don't let it get to you. You starting to get gray hairs up top."

"Yeah, Cox, tell me about it. So, what's up? You ain't come all the way down here just to tell me you saw me on *WAKE UP NEW YORK*."

"What's on your mind?"

"I might have to add more shit to your plate."

Captain Fuller stopped and looked at DA Cox.

"What are you talking about?"

"I have a guy trying to work a deal with me on a get out of jail free card. He said he knows who's running the cartel in New York and it ain't no Mexican."

"So, who the fuck is it then?"

"Ready for this one? Malachi Williams."

Captain Fuller stopped and glared at DA Cox as if he couldn't believe what he heard.

***

Malachi turned the tv off and got up from his desk and walked out his office to the main floor up to Kareem.

"We need to take a ride. It's time."

"Malachi, you sure you want to do this?" Kareem looked at Malachi as he smoked his cigar.

"My time frame is fucked up. 15 of my girls are dead. There's an investigation going on right now. Señor Blanka is calling me about this bitch on *WAKE UP NEW YORK* talking about the cartel. Am I sure that I want to do this? Let me tell you what I'm going to do. I'ma cut his chest open and take out his fucking heart and put a knife through it."

Kareem nodded. "Well Shady's been there the last few days. Give him an ass whopping. The only thing he ain't do was paint the inside walls of the room with chunks of fucking skull and blood."

Malachi smiled. "Good, it'll give me something to do."

"Malachi, stop for a second."

Malachi stopped and peered at Kareem with an inscrutable gaze.

"The man you are about to kill has been loyal to you from day one."

"Kareem, loyalty does not mean *blind obedience* to an individual. Let me ask you this, do you believe when people deserve punishment, they should be forgiven even if they are close to you and the individual who is not should be punished?"

"I'm not saying that. I'm just saying think about it before you do it."

"I did and he's a dead man. My mind is made up."

Kareem nodded as both men walked to the back of the building to the limo that was parked in the garage. The driver saw Malachi and opened the door for him to slide inside. Kareem stopped and studied him.

"We are taking a trip to Queens to the Industry Park."

"Yes sir."

Kareem stepped inside the limo. The driver closed the door and walked to the front of the limo, got in, and drove off.

Chapter 2

Shady looked at Slim as he walked to the desk in the back of the room. He sat on it and lit his blunt. Slim was tied down, bleeding from his lip and the top of his right eye were busted. He only had a pair of boxers on. Shady was pulling his blunt when Malachi and Kareem walked through the doors. Malachi strolled up to Shady and gazed at him then turned his head and looked at Slim.

"I see you leaving your company to Slim, Shady."

Shady smiled and pulled his blunt.

"Yeah, we've been playing a game called, fuck ups and the consequence behind your actions."

"Sound like fun. Are you enjoying the game?"

"Fucking right."

Malachi walked over to Slim and looked down at him. Slim glanced up at Malachi from his good eye with tears falling down his face.

"Malachi, please man. I'm sorry. Don't do this. I fucked up. It won't happen again. I swear!"

Malachi pulled a cigar out and lit it, blowing the smoke out of his mouth before talking.

"Yea, I know it won't happen again, Slim. You only had *one* job. Just drive the fucking truck to its destination, nothing else, and you fucked that up to stop by and see a bitch, long story short. You caught her with another nigga, the police get involved. You had an unregistered gun on you. Since you are a felon, you had to sit in central booking for a week. Within them seven days, my bitches died in the back of that hot ass fucking truck. Now we got this bitch on *WAKE UP NEW YORK* talking about the fucking cartel. You see what the fuck you started? A fucking domino-effect. All the fuck you need to do is say *sorry*. News flash motherfucker, human trafficking, sex trafficking, kidnapping, this ain't no damn NYPD case. It's an FBI case now. You know what type of position you put me in?"

Malachi marched up to Slim and backslapped him. "Shady, pick up the shotgun on the table and put it to his fucking face. Paint the wall behind him with chunks of his skull and fucking blood."

"Malachi, no... please. I'm sorry, man...please."

Malachi pulled his cigar and observed Slim.

"Yea, I'm sorry for trusting you, motherfucker. Shady, the walls need painting."

"About fucking time, we rock this baby to sleep."

Shady picked up the shotgun, walked to Slim, placed it to his head, and pulled the trigger, blowing his face off.

"Shady, dump the body off somewhere. Kareem, get me all the information I need on that bitch from *WAKE UP NEW YORK* and let this be a lesson that I hope I don't have to discuss with any of you."

Malachi walked out the room, leaving Kareem and Shady standing there as he made his way back to the limo. Shady looked at Kareem as he still had the shotgun in his hand.

"Kareem, did he just *threaten* us?"

"No, he just made us a *signature promise*. Take care of the body. I have some phone calls to make."

Kareem strode out the room with his phone in his hand.

***

"Now Jasmine, tell me what this meeting is about."

"Mr. Westmoreland asked me if he could get an ordinance with you today. Concerning what, I don't exactly know, but he said it was important."

"It's always important when there's money involved. He's the banker. He's going to come in here with his politics. What he can't do, and at the end of the day, he's going to need more money to get it done. That's what he going to tell me. He can't do it without more money."

"We'll see in the next few minutes. He said he will be here by noon."

Malachi looked at his watch and pulled a cigar out and lit it.

"After this meeting, I need to tell you what I need done this week."

"It's another move?"

"Yea, a big one."

Before Jasmine could reply, Mr. Westmoreland walked through the doors holding a briefcase in his hand.

"Mr. Westmoreland, it's good to see you again. Now can you tell me what was so important that you needed to see me today?"

Mr. Westmoreland opened his briefcase up and pulled some papers out and passed them to Malachi to look over.

"Mr. Williams, you have way too much money coming in. We are three times as much as before and I'm trying to keep these red flags from popping up. The only way I can do that is with more money to butter a few more people's hands to help me clean this money and make it legal."

Malachi placed the papers down on the table then looked up at Mr. Westmoreland.

"Mr. Westmoreland, how much more are you talking?"

"Five percent on every dollar."

Malachi puffed on his cigar and nodded his head.

"I'll do that with one point five million out of every six million. That should be more than enough. It was two percent before, now it's five percent."

Mr. Westmoreland looked at Malachi's demeanor on his face and nodded as a sign of agreement.

14

"Good... now that is out of the way, Mr. Westmoreland, I will have to ask you to excuse me. I have some other business to attend to."

"Sure, and I will be in touch Mr. Williams."

Malachi got up and shook his hand again before he walked out the door.

"Now that's over, Jasmine, let me tell you what is going on. Because of Slim, we have a lot of unnecessary heat on us, so we need to branch out. I'ma have Cordial and Shady go out to New Jersey and test the waters out there to set up shop and I want you and B-More to go to Philadelphia and do the same thing. Me and Kareem are going to keep things tight here just in case a motherfucker tries to get out of line."

"Are we bearing gifts when we go out there?"

"No, the only gift we bearing if they get out of line, or in our fucking way, is a *fuck you* and a first class passport to see their maker. Jasmine, we are the *BLACK DIAMOND CARTEL.* Motherfuckers are going to respect us or die. There is no other choice, hands down."

"And what are we going to do about the cartel? I think its time she sees firsthand what these girls go through." Jasmine looked pointedly at Malachi.

"Are you saying what I think you are saying?"

"Fucking right here, pussy will be on the market real soon."

Without saying another word, Malachi got up and walked out, leaving Jasmine alone with her thoughts.

Chapter 3

"Captain, come in and have a seat. I need to have a word with you."

Captain Fuller sat down in front of Chief Ward's desk and looked at Chief Ward as he placed the newspaper down on his desk.

"What can I do for you, Chief?"

"As you already know, the FBI has taken over the human trafficking case, but New York City is our backyard, so I made some calls. You will be working hand in hand with them. We need to know who is running this cartel and fucking our city up."

"Chief, after my interview with *WAKE UP NEW YORK* this morning, District Attorney Cox dropped by to see me, and he said that he got some intel from one of his informants that's why he's trying to make a deal on a get out of jail free card. For his freedom he will tell us everything we need to know about the man who is behind the drug, gun, human trafficking, and sex trafficking, he's ready to put everything on the table."

Chief Ward leaned up against his desk.

"Did he tell you who the man is behind all of this?"

"You ready for this one, Chief?"

"Fucking right."

"Malachi Williams."

"You have to be fucking kidding me, but you know what, Fuller? I can go for that shit... Malachi disappeared, but he still has his thumb firmly on New York City. A fucking *pawn* became a *king*, but before we roll the dice on this informer's information, I want everything on Malachi. Everything we have... let's see if we can connect the dots, Captain. It's time that we drown the shark."

"I'll get on it right away, Chief."

"Good, I want updates twice a day, Captain."

"Yes sir." Captain Fuller got up and walked out the chief's office with Malachi on his mind.

***

Malachi sat in the back of the limo smoking a cigar as he headed back to the office when his phone went off. He looked and seen it was Kareem calling him. He exhaled the smoke out of his mouth before picking up.

"What you have for me, Kareem?"

"I have an address on her. When do you want this to take place?"

Malachi inhaled on his cigar, "Have someone visit her tonight and Kareem, I want her stripped down on a truck tonight headed to the Bronx."

"I'll get on that now."

"Kareem, make sure nobody fucks this up because their life depends on it."

Before Kareem could say a word, Malachi hung up the phone and looked out the window as the city passed by, becoming lost in thought. He knew there was more to Stacy Hall and he was going to bring it out of her.

Chapter 4

Deputy District Attorney Cox walked into the investigation room and placed Mikey Roberto's file on the table along with a pack of cigarettes, a lighter, pulled out his seat, and looked at him.

"I'm gonna get right to the point. I want everything you have on Malachi Williams. That's the only way this deal is going to work. You said he's the head of the cartel in New York City. Well, guess what? I'm here so you can help me build my case. Now let's see how bad you want this get out of jail free card. Let's break this code of silence you stand on."

Deputy District Attorney Cox placed a tape recorder on the table and pressed record as he lit a cigarette and nodded at Mikey.

"He calls it the Black Diamond Cartel and he's plugged in directly with the Mexican Cartel Superior Blanka."

***

"I'm just getting off the train now. I'm walking out the subway now, Taylor. I'll be there in 20 minutes tops. I'll see you in a few." Stacy Hall placed her cell phone in her purse, walked up to the yellow cab, opened the door, and got inside.

"Where to?"

"106 and Park, Suite 26."

The driver pulled off after turning the meter on. Stacy Hall pulled her phone back out.

"Excuse me, you just made a right and 106 and Park is straight ahead."

"I know. They have a construction crew working two blocks up, so I'm taking this detour to save you some money and me some time. This alley brings us right on top of 106 and Park. We will be there ten minutes flat."

18

Stacy Hall didn't say anything as she continued to check her emails on her phone when a black van cut them off. Two men jumped out with assault rifles pointed at the cab. Stacy dropped her phone on the floor as they opened her cab door and pulled her out at gunpoint and dragged her to the van. The cab driver picked up her phone and jumped in the van as it pulled off.

Malachi got a text to his phone. He looked and read it with a smile on his face. It said: *Picked up package, delivering it now.* He placed his phone down and took a sip of his brandy. He then texted Kareem and said: *There's something I need to show you. Meet me at the office at 3pm. We need to take a ride somewhere.*

***

"Malachi, you know this is a big step outside of Blanka Circle. He could take this as you spitting in his face. He might take this personal."

Malachi looked at the 40 acres of farmland then back at Kareem.

"He could take this as me spitting in his face or as a win-win as long as he gets his royalties. With us growing our own cocaine plants, there's no stopping us. Kilos will be 100% pure and no longer going for $40,000, but we can drop the price to $25,000."

"Malachi, I see your vision, but if Blanka does take this as a insult, then what?"

Malachi looked at Kareem and shook his head as he looked out over the acres of land.

"You know what? Let's cross that bridge when we get there, Kareem, but look around. I have private airspace, so we don't have to worry about no commercial airplanes flying over the farm. We are deep upstate New York... miles from anybody. I have two security teams watching over the property and 20 workers on the farm. This is another step, a new beginning for us. Our very own signature on the east coast."

Kareem nodded. "What about Stacy Hall?"

Malachi lit his cigar.

"She works for me now and when I'm done with her, I'm throw that bitch's body in the trash. Now let's see what they doing in the tents. I want to show you the new stamps I'm putting on all the kilos."

***

Stacy opened her eyes. Her head was hurting where she was hit. She couldn't really see anything about her surroundings. Her eyesight was blurry. She felt her bare skin on the cold metal. Her hands were chained to the wall. After a few minutes, she saw a few females with just their bra and panties on sitting next to her on the floor. With her head bowed down, she asked, "Where am I?"

The girl looked at her, "The Diamond Playhouse."

"The Diamond Playhouse?"

Right after Stacy said that, the back of the truck's doors opened up. There were three men standing there holding assault rifles in their hands. Stacy closed her eyes because the light from outside was blinding her, it was so bright. One of the guys jumped on the back of the truck and started taking the chains off the females.

"Get up and come stand in a fucking line. Try any dumb shit and I'll kill you right fucking here. Your life ain't your life no more. I own your rights and your body."
Stacy got up and didn't say a word as she was led off the truck with the other ten females. One of the girls looked around and ran off. The guard shook his head and pulled his gun out, shooting her in the leg, causing her to fall to the ground. He nodded his head at the other guards. Everyone watched as he dragged her back by her hair back to the line.

She was yelling and screaming. As she cried out loud, the guard who shot her walked up to her and kicked her in her face three times.

"You just had to be the dumb bitch who tried me. There's always one out of the bunch."

He took his assault rifle and smacked her in the face over and over. Then he started kicking her in the stomach.

"Y'all see this bitch. Learn from her what *not* to do. You will do what you are told, or this will happen to you."

The girl laid on the ground bleeding badly, not moving. The guard put his hand up as one of the other guards handed him a machete. Everyone stood frozen in place as he swung it. Within two chops to her neck, her head was off. Stacy put her hands over her mouth and was shaking from the adrenaline coursing through her body. She couldn't believe what she just saw. She looked at the dead girl's head next to her body.

"Put her body in the grinder and feed the dogs."

Everyone gawked as he threw her head in the massive grinder. Then they tossed her body in next.

"I hope I have your attention now, so shut the fuck up and follow me."

Stacy and the rest of the girls walked inside the building. Once inside they saw females being fucked. Some were laying there like they were dead. Others were on the floor. The guard walked two females to a room and closed the door behind them. Once he was at the last room, he walked Stacy and one other girl to the last room and pushed them inside, closing the door. Stacy sat on the mattresses on the floor and just cried, hoping this was all a bad dream, but seeing these girls being fucked in other rooms, she knew exactly where she was at.

***

Shady looked around at the projects and the few people walking around as he smoked his blunt.

"Cordial, whose turf is this?"

Cordial looked at Shady.

"No one has a flag planted here. We are about to own these blocks. We have four apartments already. One to sell out of, one to bag up all the product and get it ready for the sell room. Over there, we have two apartments to watch the block to see who comes and goes. We have a 12 man team out here with us." Shady passed the blunt to Cordial.

"Shit, let's get it rocking. When is it popping off?"

Cordial smiled and looked at Shady. "It's already in motion. They just waiting on us to get here. Come on, let's make our presence be known."

Both of them walked in the project building, passing niggas and bitches on the block staring at them. Shady had his hand on his gun as he stepped up the stairs to the apartment. When Cordial knocked on the door, the peep hole slid open, and a man on the other side of the door peered out and seen it was Cordial before opening the door. Once inside Shady spotted the cocaine on the tables and the females with nothing on cutting and bagging up the kilos. Three men were walking around with assault rifles in their hands. He looked at Cordial and nodded.

Chapter 5

Blanka walked outside in the heavy rain in the middle of the garden where his mother and wife were standing under an umbrella in front of two headstones. One was his brother's and the other was his son's.

"Mama, come inside... it's raining and cold. I don't want you to get sick." Blanka pleaded as he rested his hand on her shoulder.

Without looking at him, she said, "Today makes one year that my son and your son was taken away from us by them *putas* that live in America. Feeling protected, tell me *Señor* Blanka, how does it feel to know the man who order your son's death walks around like a king while your son's bones lay still in a cold wet grave?"

Blanka's mother turned her face and looked at him as the water ran down his face.

"Tell me, son, cartels kill over cocaine, turfs, disloyalty... wars start for less. Is not my son's, your brother, your son's, my grandchild, blood worth blood in the streets? They were killed like wild cattle and here you stand doing *nothing* to avenge them."

"Mama, my hands are tied. There's no proof that Manny's cartel have they blood on his hands."

Blanka's mother looked at the black limo pulling up to the back of the house.

"My hands are not tied even if Manny's cartel didn't have nothing to do with their deaths, they blood will be spilled for it."

Blanka gazed at his mother as she pulled a knife out and cut the middle of her right hand. As the blood oozed from the wound, she let it run over both her son's and grandson's headstones. Blanka looked at the limo.

"Mama, who is in the limo? What have you done?"

Blanka's mother smiled as she looked at the limo doors opening, and Malachi stepped out and walked towards them under an umbrella.

"Mama, no."

Blanka's mother placed the hand she cut on his cheek and let the blood drip down his chin.

"It's too late. My blood is already spilled."

Malachi walked up to them, shook Blanka's hand, kissed his wife's hand, and kissed his mother on the cheek.

"Mrs. Blanka, you requested my presence immediately. I'm here at your request."

She walked up to Malachi and hugged him. "I called you here for a blood oath. I need you to pledge your loyalty here today in front of Blanka, Angie, myself, and my loved one's graves. My house, my cartel opened the door to New York City for you today. I ask you to spill your blood for my house."

Malachi looked at the blood on her hand and the bloody knife in the other hand. He never took his eyes off of her as he took the knife from her and cut the middle of his hand. She took his hand and held it over both headstones and let the blood drip down on them. Then she placed her hand on top of his and looked into his eyes.

"Manny Moreno is the head of the cartel in Texas. Bring me his body dead or alive so I can lay his body right next to my son and grandson."

"I will." Malachi kissed the blood on her hand as a seal of loyalty, knowing loyalty comes with a price.

"Come Malachi, there's much you need to know about him."

She led Malachi into the house. Blanka looked at his wife standing in the rain, looking at her son's headstone.

"This could end very badly, Angie."

24

Angie walked up to Blanka and looked into his eyes. "Sometimes, only death can claim justice, in this case, *revenge*… let death collect her number and have her sweet victory. Let's take our revenge."

Angie walked away, leaving Blanka standing at the headstones, viewing the blood of his mother's and Malachi's that was spilled on them. Knowing they were going to war now, but even deeper secrets may come to light before everything is said and done.

***

"Captain Fuller, we have a missing person case."

Captain Fuller looked up at the officer at his office door as she was holding a file in her hand. He placed his coffee down on his desk and waved her inside his office.

"Who is the missing person and why are you bringing it to me and not the missing person department?"

"Because the person who is missing, I thought you might want to know."

"Who is it?"

"Stacy Hall from WAKE UP NEW YORK."

Captain Fuller couldn't believe what he just heard. He leaned against his desk and reached for the file in her hand.

"When was she reported missing and by who?" Captain Fuller asked as he looked over the details in the file.

"The call came in two days ago by a Mr. Kevin Taylor, but we couldn't file the report for 72 hours, sir."

"When was the last time she was seen?" he questioned.

"The day you did your interview, sir, on *WAKE UP NEW YORK*. He said around five p.m., she called him and told him she was just getting off the train and she will see him in 20 minutes. He haven't heard from her since."

"Have a car go out to her house. Get her phone records. I want to know who was the last person she talked to and see if we can get the last location on her phone, officer."

"Yes sir."

Captain Fuller picked up the phone and called Deputy District Attorney Cox. After a few rings someone picked up and patched him through to the DA's office.

"Cox, It's Fuller."

"I'm glad you called. I went in and talked to the informant. There's a few things I need to run by you."

"Yeah, because we have a big fucking problem. I hope your informer is the real deal because Stacy Hall was just reported missing."

District Attorney Cox took his hand and ran it down his face.

"I'm on my way now to see you, Fuller."

"I'll see you when you get here, Cox." Captain Fuller hung up the phone and walked to the chief's office. There was no hiding the truth now. It was out and Stacy Hall had exposed it. The cartel was in New York City, and she just became a victim to it.

Chapter 6

Stacy Hall watched as the door opened and the man who killed the girl was standing there looking at her with a machete in his hand.

"I'm only going to say this one time. Don't make me repeat myself and don't repeat the same mistake the other girl made because I'm not going to kill you. I'm going to cut one of your fingers off and one of your ears the first time you disobey me. The second time, I'm removing one of your eyes and three more of your fingers. Do I make myself clear?"

Stacy Hall had tears coming down her face as she nodded at him.

"Good. I'm taking you to another room and you will put on what I provide for you. A man wearing a mask will come in there and you will make him see stars for 45 minutes. After he leaves, you will wash up and that will be your new room. Don't ask no questions. Just do what I tell you to do. I know *everything* that goes on in here. Don't make me bring you in front of all the girls and do horrible things to you, because *I will*. Now come on. It's showtime."

Stacy got up and followed him down the hall to a nicer room. She looked at the bed and saw a red, lace two-piece with black and red heels on the floor.

"You have 30 minutes to get cleaned up. I'll be back to check on you then."

She looked at the man as he walked out the room, closing the door behind him.

***

Malachi had two stress balls in his hand as he rode to the airport to his private jet. Mrs. Blanka asked him to kill Manny Moreno. She told him Manny controlled one of the biggest cartels in Texas. Not only was he well protected by the FBI, he was one of the biggest confidential informants.

Killing him would be like trying to find a needle in a haystack, but he told her anybody can be killed. It's all throughout history. JFK, Caesar, Malachi knew it only took one weak link and even the biggest ship would sink. Malachi became a monster to sit at the table with monsters. He pulled out a cigar and lit it. Blanka didn't talk to him much about Manny being brought back alive. He stressed a dead corpse being brought back to an open grave. If Malachi rolled the dice and beat that, Blanka had his brother's blood on his hands, and Manny been keeping a secret. Malachi stepped out of the limo and boarded the plane, knowing that one open grave may hold two bodies soon. If the dice that Malachi rolled against Blanka was true.

***

"Shady, strap up and come on. We have visitors."

Shady cocked his 9mm and walked out the apartment door behind Cordial, heading down the hall to the apartment lobby where they had four guards standing in front of three dudes from the other side of the block. When Cordial and Shady stalked up to them, they were face to face with all three dudes.

"Who the fuck are you niggas?" Cordial asked.

"We the niggas that want to know who the fuck green lighted y'all to open shop on this block?"

"Do you know who the fuck we are? Green lighted, nigga, we Timberland stomp where the fuck we want to and body any niggas that cross our fucking path who want to be tough guys."

"Newsflash motherfucker. Pat is giving you 24 hours to shut this shit down or we going to see them bodies drop and see who really are the tough guys around here."

"Nigga, we ain't shutting *shit* down. Fuck Pat. Matter of fact, tell that nigga Cordial said to suck dick. Now y'all niggas get the fuck out my building and off my block before y'all be the first bodies to drop."

Shady walked up front for Cordial and pulled his 9mm out and grilled them as they took two steps back and backed off. One of them pointed his finger at Shady.

"Come on, Cordial. Fuck them soft ass niggas."

Cordial looked at his three guards standing there. "If them niggas come back, flatline they ass. Mix they blood with mud."

Cordial and Shady walked back into the building.

***

Stacy looked at the white heavyset man with the mask over his face as he walked into the room. He examined her as she stood there with a two piece on. Stacy turned her head as a tear came down her face, knowing that what she did at that moment her life depended on it. She wiped the tear from her eye and walked over to the man and started unbuttoning his shirt. As she was taking it off, he grabbed her hands and lowered her on the floor. As he unbuttoned his pants and pulled his pants and boxers off, Stacy grabbed his penis and started jerking it off.p

"Put it in your mouth, now."

Stacy looked up at him as he said that before she opened her mouth and started to suck on him, prompting his penis to grow in her mouth. He had his hand on the back of her head, putting his whole seven inches in her mouth.

"Yeah, just like that. Keep going... don't stop."

Stacy was sucking and licking all over his manhood as she played with his balls. He started fucking her face hard. He held her head still as he let out a walnut in her mouth. He let his manhood rest on her tongue as his hands were still on the back of her head.

"Swallow everything then get on the bed."

Stacy did as she was told, getting on the bed in the doggy style position as he grabbed her waist and slid inside of her. Stacy placed her head on the pillow as a tear came down her face.

Chapter 7

"Cox, before we start, how reliable is this informant you are working with?"

Deputy District Attorney Cox opened his briefcase up and pulled a file out.

"He very reliable and he just gave us the icing on the cake and the match to light the dry grass to a blaze."

Captain Fuller lit a cigarette and picked up the file Cox placed on the desk.

"So, who is the guy and how come he knows so much?"

"You remember Green who used to work for Peter Drews, his body was put in the trunk of a car in a New Jersey junkyard?"

"Yeah, two of my detectives had it on film when they raided their spots. One went out with a shoot out getting himself killed and the other one we got coming out of a sports bar. He didn't put up a fight. That was an easy bust."

"That's right, Fuller, and he gave us so much information over the last years. We had to move him out of state prison under a fake name. That's how deep his mob ties go."

Captain Fuller pulled on his cigarette.

"So, what is he putting on the table for this get out of prison free card? He hired a hitman out of organized crime. This has got to be good."

"Fuller, he gave us something better than a 21 year old girl wet tight cookie."

Both men started laughing. District Attorney Cox placed a tape recorder on the desk and pressed play as he lit his own cigarette.

"This is Deputy District Attorney Cox. I'm interviewing informer John Doe identification number 1076243. This interview is on Malachi Williams. Now tell me what you have on Malachi Williams after you state your name for the record?"

"This is John Doe, id number 1076243. Malachi Williams is the head of the Black Diamond Cartel operating in New York City all the way to the west coast. His major supplier is Señor Blanka over the Mexican cartel. Blanka ships over 2 tons of cocaine, X pills, heroin, and a new drug called Ky that's killing people."

"How do you know all of this because our intel tells us Malachi Williams hasn't been seen in New York City in over a year? He is like a ghost to us right now."

"That's the best way to be, Deputy District Attorney Cox. You can't stop what you can't see."

"What do you mean, you can't stop what you can't see?"

"I guess I'ma have to spell everything out for y'all. All this time he had reconstructive surgery on his face and voice box. The man you know as Malachi Williams doesn't look the same or sound the same. He even have a new government name. He could walk right up to you and ask you for a cigarette and you will never know it was him."

Captain Fuller couldn't believe what he was hearing.

"So how can we get in touch with him?"

"You can't. He has people that reach out to you. No one talks to him face to face or directly but the cartel."

"How do I know you ain't feeding me a bunch of bullshit? This could be a fairy tale of the do you mean boogeyman. You have to give me something to back all of this up."

"Let me tell you what I want. I want an attorney with a signed agreement from the governor for my immediate release under protected custody and this is what I will do. I will give you his main contact and you can connect the dots from there because when this gets out, there will be a death certificate waiting on my body. The only question you need to ask yourself Deputy District Attorney Cox, deal or no deal?"

District Attorney Cox cut the tape recorder off and looked at Captain Fuller.

"Before you say anything, I pulled a few strings and called in a few favors. His story about Malachi Williams checks out about the surgery and new name."

"You have to be fucking kidding me. All this time he was right under our nose and the interview with Stacy Hall got her kidnapped. Come on... we have to run this by my captain."

***

Malachi walked in the office where he had everyone waiting on him, dressed in all black, sitting at the table as his two pit bulls walked around the office checking for any perceived threats. He sat at the head of the table and lit a cigar before talking.

"As we grow as the first black cartel, everyday we have to move smarter. We don't only have to think for ourselves but for our enemies as well. I only trust the people at this. With that being said, everyone here's loyalty is deeper and thicker than black blood. Jasmine, I need you to go to Texas. There's a man who's named Manny. He is the head of the cartel down there. Not only that, he has the FBI watching over him. He is one of their superstar informers, but he also has Blanka's son's and brother's blood on his hand. I was just called in on a favor over that. They want Manny dead or alive. Bring him back to them on a blood plaque. I just need you to get him somewhere away from his cartel and FBI agents. Make sure you change your appearance."

Jasmine nodded at Malachi.

"Kareem, I need you here running things in New York. I'm going to Texas with Jasmine. Cordial, we don't need bodies dropping right now but do what you have to do. We are not giving no blocks back. Shady, I want you with him every step of the way but be ready to move if Kareem calls you. We have the east coast in a headlock right now. We have over 40 workers moving cocaine, X pills, KY heroin, trafficking… everything from guns and drugs to people. We have our own cocaine farm. There is no stopping us. We have the keys to the city. Them noodle eating motherfuckers know what line to cross and not to cross. We haven't had a problem out of them in over two years. They got the picture we painted for them in blood as long as we stay loyal to each other. There is no stopping us."

Malachi walked to the bar and got a bottle of Circo and five glasses and poured everyone a shot.

"We drinking to loyalty but most importantly to family."

Everyone raised their glasses and drank to family.

***

Manny strode up to his prize winning racehorse and rubbed his head. As he was standing in the stable, Manny watched as his second in command, Cruise, walked up to him.

"You know there's something us gamblers say, 'if there is a winner, there is a loser.' I'm willing to bet this horse paid for himself over 100 times already. Just look at him. Just to breed him, I'm asking $10,000. His bloodline is worth it. Come talk to me. What brings you down here?"

"Our clients in California are asking for twice the amount on the next shipment and to confirm Jason White is coming to Texas today to have a late dinner with you at Fabio's at 9pm tonight. I need the green light from you about the meeting tonight."

Manny walked out of the stable and lit a cigar and looked up at his horse track.

"Set the meeting up. Have two security teams with us, no more than 4 guards."

"I'll let him know right now, Manny, and I'll get the detail ready for tonight."

Cruise walked off as Manny waved to his wife who was riding a white Appaloosa he got for their anniversary last year.

Chapter 8

"Malachi, we went from corners and blocks, to private planes, to cocaine farms, to supplying the east coast."

Malachi looked at Jasmine and nodded as he lit his cigar. They were on a private plane headed to Texas.

"We have come a long way, Jasmine. We lost and gained a lot but remember we are still little dogs in a big dog's game. Once I get out from underneath Señor Blanka's wing, we can branch out how I want us to."

"So how do you plan on getting to Manny if he's protected the way you said?"

"I reached out to a contact in California and called in a favor for a favor. He's meeting Manny tonight at Fabio's restaurant to discuss new business. I want to see his security detail and then we will go from there."

Jasmine didn't say anything else. She sipped on her glass of wine and put her trust in Malachi as she knew he was in deep thought. She knew he wouldn't bring her to a fight if he knew they couldn't win.

***

Manny watched as his wife swam in their in-ground swimming pool in the house as he smoked his cigar getting ready to leave for his meeting with Jason White. He had two cars and a four man security detail waiting on him outside. He turned around and walked up to Cruise.

"Where are we sitting at in the restaurant?"

"The back table. It's private and already reserved for us. We need to get moving before we are late getting there, sir."

Manny pulled his cigar and walked over to the black Range Rover where one of the guards opened the door for him to get in with Cruise trailing along right behind him.

"Cruise, this could be big if White is trying to expand in California and they said you can't have your cake and eat it too."

Señor smiled after saying that. Both Range Rovers pulled up in front of the restaurant. Manny stepped out with his men. He looked around before walking in the restaurant to the table where Jason White and two of his men were waiting on him. Señor Cruise strolled up to him with a smile on his face as they shook hands and hugged. Malachi watched with Jasmine from a few tables down.

"What's your thoughts, Malachi?" Jasmine asked him as he started eating her food.

"Manny is a dinosaur, and we are the comet coming straight at him that he doesn't even see coming. He is so into White he does his song and dance for me. He has a four man security detail. Two black Range Rovers, he's relaxed, but not comfortable. Come on, let's get out of here. I want to see the way he drives home."

***

Blanka looked at his mother from the deck's glass doors as she lit two candlesticks outside on the deck in the garden underneath the statue of Santa Maria as she said prayers to her son. He knew his mother mourned for her lost son. His wife put her hand on his shoulder, getting his attention.

"Your mother mourns deeply for him. The time for grief is over, Blanka. It's time for Manny to lay next to your brother and our son in a cold wet grave."

Blanka looked at his wife and grabbed her hand and kissed it.

"Death comes with a price, dear. We have no proof that Manny has their blood on his hands."

Angie looked in Blanka's eyes before speaking, "Then we kill to find out who does. Blood is the only justice for our loss right now. Let Santa Maria claim Manny's soul, my love."

Angie kissed his cheek and sauntered off, leaving him to over watch his mother's prayers.

Chapter 9

"You let this nigga named Cordial come to our city and take bread out of our mouths then he going to tell *you* to tell *me* to 'suck his dick.' What the fuck is wrong with you? Why you ain't roll his ass when he was talking sideways out his fucking mouth."

Pat was in Black Rob's face on the project steps a few blocks from Cordial's blocks.

"Them niggas was holding. They was all gripping toast."

"So, what the fuck? You weren't holding? You tucked your tail and ran. These out of state niggas are still eating and y'all niggas are posted up like shit just going to blow over? Get the fuck off the steps. Grab the burners and let them New York cats say, *'what's up to y'all little friends.'* Y'all mother fuckers ain't getting no cake to them. Niggas are rolled now. Step the fuck off the block and go body a nigga."

Pat watched them walk off as he lit his blunt.

***

Kareem stepped out the car and walked into the Diamond Playhouse. All eyes were on him as he walked through the hallway talking on his phone.

"I'm here checking on her now. Are you sure the farm? Ok then, I'm going to talk with Derrick now and I'll call you back and tell you how she's holding up."

Kareem hung up the phone with Malachi as he walked up to Derrick.

"How is our celebrity doing?"

"She finally getting the picture of how things work in this house. She seen three top rate customers within the last week."

Kareem nodded and lowered his head as he lit his cigar. "Take me to her."

Derrick walked Kareem to Stacy's room. Kareem looked at her through the window on the door as she sat on the bed with her head in her hands while rocking back and forth on the bed.

"Just like Malachi wanted, Kareem, a nice room to make her feel comfortable as possible."

Kareem didn't say a word. He just opened the door and walked into the room. Stacy looked up at him then over at Derrick. She stood up and started to get undressed. Kareem put his hands up to stop her.

"Leave us. I'll see you in a few." Kareem said, looking at Derrick.

Derrick didn't say a word as he walked out the room, closing the door behind him. Stacy looked at Kareem, taking stock of how he was well-dressed in a three piece suit to his curly jet black hair, dark brown eyes, and impeccably groomed goatee. She knew he was a man of power.

"Do you know why you are here? Why this is happening to you?"

Stacy said with tears in her eyes, "Yes and I'm so sorry. Please can I go home? I will never talk about the cartel again. I swear."

Kareem puffed on his cigar and scanned her seriously then shook his head.

"Stacy Hall, your mother of four children lives at 220 Maple Avenue. She has been living there for the last 30 years. Your sister and her husband live in South Side Jamaica Queens with their 3 children, ages 12, 10, 3. Your little brother plays basketball for UCLA, point guard. Your father works downtown. He's a forklift operator."

Stacy couldn't believe what she was hearing.

"Stacy, I killed more people than John Gotti at the height of his career in the Gambino family and in the worst ways, from skinning them alive to putting rats in a bucket on their stomachs and putting a flame on the bucket. The rat eats through their stomach to get away from the flame. I put bricks on chains and tied them to motherfuckers and threw them in the East River. I say all of this because I don't see your tears or hear your cries. I'm here to give you a choice. You can stay here and get fucked or you can come work on the farm. The choice is yours, but if you come to the farm and try and run, I will kill your whole fucking family in the worst way. I'll record it and put it online so the world will see it after I make your mother fuck until her pussy starts to bleed. I'm not to be fucked with."

Stacy nodded, looking at Kareem.

"Can I go to the farm please?"

"Yeah."

Kareem went to leave the room when Stacy asked him, "Will I ever have a chance to go back home?"

"From this point on, that's up to you. I'll be back in a few minutes."

Kareem walked out the room and called Malachi back.

***

Shady walked out the project building, dapping one of the guys out front as he lowered his head to light his blunt. His phone went off and seen it was Cordial calling. He drew on the blunt before picking up the phone.

"Yoo, what's rocking, fam?"

"I'm just checking on how we are looking up there, playboy."

"Like butter, it's smooth on this end. I'm outside smoking a blunt while they count the cake upstairs, baby."

"Say no less, be on point. I'm touching down over there tomorrow morning, if not tonight."

"Copy that." Shady hung up the phone with Cordial and relit his blunt. Shady started bopping his head when one of the guys started playing 50 Cent's *My Toy Soldier* out the apartment window as he started singing along with the song.

"I put that batter in his back. I'm the reason why he move like that. That's my motherfucking toy soldier. I tell pop that gat he's going to pop that gat."

Shady was so into the song, he didn't see two dudes walking up with their hoodies on towards him, guns clasped in their hand as they pointed the guns at him. Noticing the out of place guys and sensing what's about to go down, looking out for his guy, Wild Style called Shady's name, causing him to drop his blunt as Wild Style jumped in front of him. The unknown dudes starting firing their guns at him, with Wild Style getting shot in the back and the side. Shady had pulled his gun out and started shooting back at them while on the ground, hitting one of the guys in the chest as he took off running. Shady got up and took off running behind them. The one guy who got shot in the chest fell down, dropping his gun. Shady kicked him in the face, making him roll over on his back. Shady pointed the gun at his face and fired two rounds in his head, killing him instantly. Looking up, he saw the black car peeling off the block. Three of Shady's guys ran outside to him and Shady looked at them.

"Get this body the fuck up out of here." Shady marched back to the back of the project where Wild Style was laying on the ground with two guys standing over him. Wild Style stared at Shady one last time before he closed his eyes for the final curtain. Shady shook his head and bit his bottom lip before walking off enraged. Heads were gonna roll for this one.

***

Malachi's car pulled up at the Apple Mount range. He stepped out with Jasmine and looked around. One of Jason's men walked up to him and Jasmine.

"Mr. Malachi, can you please follow me?"

Malachi nodded and followed the man to the apple patch where Jason White was sitting under an apple tree drinking a glass of wine and eating out of a fruit basket. Jason got up and shook Malachi's hand and did the same thing with Jasmine.

"Malachi, it's good to see you again, you as well Jasmine."

"Always a pleasure, Jason," Jasmine said.

"Likewise, Jason."

"Malachi, tell me, what has you so interested in Manny that you called in a favor on a dead locket with me?"

Malachi looked at Jason. "How about we share a cigar and I'll tell you."

Jason nodded as Malachi passed him a Cuban cigar.

"I was called in on a blood oath from Señor Blanka's mother two weeks ago. She believes that Manny has her son's blood on his hands and she wants his body in a grave."

Malachi showed Jason his hand where the cut was at.

"You know Malachi, there are so many rumors about that and a rumor without proof is just an empty claim."

Jason pulled his cigar and looked at Malachi.

"Malachi, loyalty comes with a price and I'm walking out on the limb with what I'm about to tell you. What I'm about to say ain't no rumor or empty claim. It's a *cold hard fact* but for that information, you will supply me at half the price I'm getting from Manny with 100% pure."

Malachi looked at Jasmine.

"I have no problem with that, but you will help me secure the package. I'm not going under $16,000 on each kilo."

"I can work with that. You know some stories you just don't repeat, like when you were a kid, you were afraid to say "Boogeyman" three times because he might just come out of your closet and get your ass. That's one of these type of stories. Malachi, there's more than just Blanka's brother's blood on Manny's hands. Blanka has *the same* blood on *his* hands too."

Malachi pulled on his cigar and looked squarely in Jason's eyes when he said that.

"What do you mean, Blanka has the same red blood on his hands?"

Jason took a sip of his wine then puffed on his cigar. "Rumors were already in the air that Manny was an informant working with the FBI. Blanka didn't want no dealings with Manny because let's face it, a rat is a fucking rat and dealing with Manny is bad for business. That could cause a chain reaction, but what Blanka didn't know was that Keko was going to confront Manny about the rumors. Manny was already upset because Keko stopped Manny's orders until Manny explained the rumors involving the FBI. That led to a very disrespectful phone conversation and some words you just can't take back. Manny had it already set up to where Manny's men were going to shoot the car up, so when Keko's car pulled up, shots were fired. Rumor has it that the only one who was shot was Blanka's son. Besides the driver, Keko didn't get hit. Keko brought Blanka's son as a witness to the conversation. Keko's driver took off but he didn't make it ten minutes down the street. He lost a lot of blood and lost control of the car, hitting a gate. Keko jumped out the car with Blanka's son's blood all over him. He ran to the front of the car and pulled his driver out, but when he turned around the black SUV pulled up and there were men who jumped out with assault rifles. The whole armor of God couldn't protect him at that moment in time. How they left his body, he was *unrecognizable*. One of the men ran to the back of the car and looked in before getting back in the SUV as it pulled off."

Jason took a sip of his drink and pulled on his cigar before talking again. Malachi paid close attention to the story.

44

"So, if Manny's men killed them, how does Blanka have Keko's blood on his hands? Where does Blanka fit into this?"

"The men that pulled up in the SUV were *Blanka's men* not Manny's. In Blanka's eyes, if his brother knew that Manny was an informant for the FBI and he still was working with him, then how could he be trusted? Blanka put the cartel before his brother and had him killed, not knowing his actions killed his son. *He* is the reason his son and brother are dead. Malachi, it was a double hit. Manny nor Blanka knew that they pressed the button on Keko the same day. Keko and Blanka's son's blood are on Manny's *and* Blanka's hands.

"Fuck... that's deep. How do you know all of this?"

"A drunk Manny... he was watching everything from his location with a pair of binoculars. Once they killed Keko, Blanka's men drove up the street where there was a black on black Range Rover. They told them in the Range Rover. The Range Rover drove down the street and Blanka jumped out and ran to the back of the limo where his dead son was at. He pulled his son out, but it was too late. The deed was done. His disloyalty to his brother and loyalty to the cartel killed his son. That's something he will have to live with for the rest of his life."

"Damn, he got his son's blood on his hands and Manny is holding that over his head."

"Sometimes, that's the way the cookie crumbles. The question is, what are you going to do with the knowledge now?"

"Honor my blood oath."

"Indeed you are."

Chapter 10

"Chief Ward, you and Captain Fuller along with District Attorney Cox just cracked the egg we couldn't. Malachi Williams is behind the Black Diamond Cartel sweeping throughout the East Coast, but we all know we need more than a convict's word. We need proof."

"Agent Miller, what about the disappearance of Stacy Hall? She's been missing over two weeks now and it's funny how it was right after the interview with Captain Fuller that she goes missing."

"Chief Ward, we traced her cell phone records and checked with her family and friends. We have people looking for her, but right now, we are doing nothing more than witch hunting."

"What about the U-Haul? What fingerprints did we get off that?"

"The only fingerprints we got off the U-Haul truck belong to a Micheal Bell, and we found his body missing half his head two weeks ago. Chief Ward, we are dealing with professionals. They know how to cover their tracks."

"Then we don't have a choice than to make a deal with District Attorney Cox's informer. If we have to sign a deal with a demon to catch the devil, let's roll the dice and take our chances."

"District Attorney Cox, make the deal and the only way this is going to work is if we get locations and addresses. Let's show Malachi Williams what happens when he is facing the greatest law enforcement force in the world because we just don't knock. We come in."

***

Kareem's door opened to the Maybach. He eyed Stacy sitting next to him as he took her blindfold off, and stepped outside the car. Stacy stepped out right behind him. Kareem looked at her.

"Follow me."

Stacy glanced at the men wearing all black with face masks on where you can only see their eyes as they walked around with assault rifles in their hands. She followed Kareem into the building to a private room.

"Close the door and have a seat."

Stacy did as she was told. Kareem lit a cigar and walked to the window and pulled it up. Then he went and took his seat behind the desk.

"There has been an angel watching over you. Count your blessings. Stacy, we kill people just for looking at us wrong. What you did, we would of killed your whole family just for talking about the cartel, but my boss doesn't want you dead. Instead, he wanted you to see what those girls go through firsthand. Then he told me to bring you here so now you have a choice. You can work for us willingly up here or forcefully back where you just came from, but as of today, you are a part of the Black Diamond Cartel. If you fuck us, you will pay with your life." Kareem pulled on his cigar.

"I'm going to work willingly here."

"Good... you see that room right there, there's a shower in there and a fresh change of clothes. You have 20 minutes. Go clean yourself up. I'll be right here when you get out."

Stacy got up and went in the room, closing the door behind her. She walked to the sink and looked in the mirror at her reflection as she rested her hands on the sink and started crying, knowing she crossed the line. Her boss told her not to do that interview and she still poked the bear.

***

"Man, what the fuck happened up here last night that caused Wild Style to be carried out in a black bag?"

"Pat's niggas came up clapping, no talking, just blazing right after I hung up the phone with you. Sparks were flashing and bullets flying. Wild Style took two shells for me. I bodied one of them fuck boys. The homies cleaned the body up. Cor, don't act like we didn't know them niggas wasn't going to come back. We were super disrespectful. We just didn't know they were going to come back that fast, cock locked, and ready to rock."

"Look, the block is bleeding right now. Shit is flaming hot, but when it rains, it pours and you can't stop the rain. It's time to cut these niggas' water off. We ride out tonight."

Cordial looked at everyone in the room after saying that.

"Shady, come over here and let me holla at you one on one, come talk to me private one on one."

***

Manny and his four guards walked to the back of the restaurant. Manny was drinking a glass of champagne. He had on a white dress shirt with white dress pants and white shoes. His shirt's top three buttons were unbuttoned, showing off part of his chest with gold chains around his neck. His hair was jet black with curls. He was watching the show the cook was putting on at the back of the restaurant on the grill with the food. Jasmine looked at Manny from the far part of the restaurant. She knew he was very dangerous. Jason told her and Malachi stories of people he killed in the worst way and kids were no exception— from throwing them off buildings to a bullet to the head. Jason told her and Malachi he would be here at 9pm. tonight. This was a place where he felt comfortable and relaxed. Not only was he protected by his men, but he had two police escorts with him. Jasmine got up from the table and walked to the back of the restaurant, all eyes were on her as she walked past the people clustered

48

around the luxurious tables. Her hair was honey blonde with curls coming down her face. Her eyes were light brown. She wore a tight cream dress, showing off her hourglass figure with diamond cuts on the side of the dress and a slit going up her right thigh with a diamond dog chain around her neck. She wore two inch red bottom shoes. Her mere presence made people look at her. She was a few feet away from Manny, looking at the show as well. Malachi was at the upper part of the restaurant sitting down, smoking a cigar, watching her every move. Jasmine caught Manny's attention. He walked past his guards and up to her. He whispered in a deeply accented voice, "Are you enjoying the show?"

Jasmine smiled as she looked into his eyes.

"Yes, it is amazing what he's doing with the food."

"It is, but the taste is even more amazing as the food practically melts in your mouth."

Jasmine smiled as he was talking to her.

"I'm being rude. Let me introduce myself, Manny Moreno."

"It's nice to meet you, Manny. My name is Mya Fajita."

Manny stuck his hand out to shake hers.

"Your hands are so soft, Mya... how about you come back to my table so we can enjoy an expensive meal together? I would like the opportunity to get to know you."

"I would like that, Manny. I would like to get to know you too."

Manny placed his hand on her back and led her to his table. Malachi got up and walked to the far end of the restaurant, following them from the upper level.

***

Stacy walked out of the room looking beautiful. Malachi held nothing back when he had Jasmine pick out her clothes. She looked like an upcoming queen pin. Kareem smiled when he looked at her. He walked up to her, with a little black box in his hand. He opened it and pulled out a diamond chain and placed it around her neck, looking into her eyes.

"Stacy, welcome to the Black Diamond Cartel— from being kidnapped to being placed in the Diamond Playhouse for two weeks, from going through what you went through, from standing in front of me right now. You have been gorilla bred into this cartel. You are one of *us* now. Now come on."

Stacy couldn't believe this was happening to her. She crossed the line and there was no turning back now. Kareem escorted her to a room where there were five guards walking around with guns and five tables with four nude females on each table, cutting, weighing, and bagging up the kilos of cocaine. Kareem looked down at them as he smoked his cigar. All eyes were on Stacy as she and Kareem stood on the warehouse room floor.

"Stacy, we all have a part to play in the cartel. That's how we keep things running smoothly. Violence is the recipe for success. There is no other option. Honestly, you are supposed to be at one of these table doing what you see them doing now, but Malachi wanted you where you are standing now. He sees something in you. Blanka wanted you dead. Malachi wanted you alive. This is a blessing and a curse. It's a blessing because you are alive. It's a curse because you are now a part of what you talked so negative about during your latest segment on *Wake Up New York*. Everyone in this room works for you now. Your job is to count all the product. Make sure things are ready to be shipped out on time. Watch the girls. If they fuck up, they die. No exceptions Stacy, none. I'm leaving you here. The office we were just in is yours."

Kareem passed her a phone.

"My number is in there just in case you need to reach me. Let me stress this to you. We have FBI agents, DEA agents, NYPD officers, judges, and District Attorneys working for us. If you try to fuck us, the things we will do to you and your family, they haven't invented words for. Take the blessing. I promise you, you will see the brighter side to this real soon."

Kareem waved one of the females up to him. He looked at her as she reached them.

"Kimberly, this is Stacy. Stacy, this is Kimberly. Kimberly will show you the ropes and how things work on the floor. She been with us for a while. Kimberly take care of the new boss."

Kareem looked at both of them and walked out the doors. Malachi didn't trust the police so there were no DA, judges, FBI agents, or cops working for them. He said what he had to in order to put fear in Stacy.

* * *

Shady pulled the murder one mask over his face and cocked back a Mac-11 he had in his hand. He looked at Cordial holding the M-16 and Pop-Off had a Mossberg pump. Pop-Off passed Shady the blunt. Shady pulled it twice before passing it back. The van rode down the block with the side door open. C-Murder was playing in the background. Mihita Pat was walking out of the barbershop doors, talking to a few of his guys, smiling with his back to the barbershop. When he turned around all you could hear was the sound of gunshots, glass breaking, and bullet casings dropping on the ground. Pat took three shots from the Mac-11, dropping him in front of the barbershop.

Shady yelled out. "What's up now, motherfucker? Let's play!"

As he let the Mac-11 ring, Pop-Off jumped out of the van. One of Pat's men went to run. Pop-Off shot him dead center in the chest with his Mossberg pump, blowing him through the barbershop window. Cordial walked up to Pat and looked down at him on the ground. He stood over Pat and as he held the M-16 in his hands. Pat was on the ground with blood coming out his mouth, trying to catch his breath.

"Motherfucker, y'all wanted smoke in the kitchen. Well, we're here to burn this motherfucker down."

Shady ran next to Cordial. Cordial looked at Shady and nodded. Both of them let their guns rain down on Pat, leaving his body with multiple holes. They jumped back in the van and took off, leaving Pat and his three men laid out in pools of their own blood.

Chapter 11

"Kareem, we had to strike back. They drew first blood. Niggas came clamping, no talking. Sometimes you can't stop the rain. Shit just got to pop. We made a thunderstorm and wet everyone."

"Cordial, bodies mean police investigation. Which is shit we don't need right now."

"So, what? Wild Style get bodied. Niggas take head shots at Shady, and we just lay in the cut like a Band-Aid? Kareem, my gun go off and my murder game is A1. You right, we don't need the police investigation shit right now, but if we would of let that shit ride, we would of opened the door for another goofy ass nigga to try some shit. Kareem, we from New York. Brooklyn to the jungle. Lions, tigers, and bears and we don't go for no weird shit."

"Cordial, I hear what you are saying. Big facts. Just tighten up out here and another thing, nigga, I'm not from Brooklyn. I'm from South Side Jamaica Queens, Gangsta Paradise. Get it right. I'm just eating in Brooklyn right now."

Both of them started laughing as they dapped each other up.

"So, plug me on Stacy. How's that looking upstate New York?"

"She good bred but look, I'm about to bounce. Understand Shay is young, and he looks up to you. Don't crash him out."

"Copy that fam."

"Where that nigga at anyway?"

"Counting the cake in the back."

"Sayless, tell him I came through."

Kareem looked around before leaving the apartment.

***

Malachi looked out the window to the penthouse at the city sprawled out before him. He only had a pair of sweatpants on and some red Timberland boots. He was drinking a cup of coffee when he heard a knock on the door. He s over to the table and picked up his gun and walked to the door, putting his ear to it.

"Who is it?"

"Jasmine."

Malachi opened the front door and let her inside. She looked at him. She always loved Malachi from day one. She always kept her feelings to herself but couldn't help looking at his chocolate skin tone, dark brown eyes, deep waves, broad shoulders, chest, and six pack. She loved the tattoo of the pit-bull on his side with the broken chains and paw prints going up his side to his shoulders and chest. Malachi walked backed to the table, placing his gun down. He picked up his cup of coffee and looked at Jasmine.

"How did you sleep last night, Jasmine?"

"Good, relaxed, and comfortable. What about you?"

"Peaceful, tell me about Manny."

Malachi took a sip of his coffee. Jasmine knew she was a bad bitch. She ambled up to Malachi, taking his cup and placing it back down on the table. She wrapped her arms around his neck and gazed into his eyes, knowing she was about to cross the line and break all the rules. She knew it was something they both wanted.

"Malachi, let's not play with each other no more."

Jasmine kissed Malachi on the lips as he picked her up and carried her to the bedroom, laying her down on the bed as SWV was playing in the background. Malachi pulled her red bottom shoes off and started kissing her feet, pushing her dress up her thighs as he kissed her legs, going up her thighs slow and gentle till he found her honey pot. Jasmine was letting out soft tight moans from Malachi's touch. He pulled her thong down and placed his tongue on her clit and licked her in circles as his tongue found the inside of her. He wrapped his arms around her legs, pulling her closer to him as she was grinding her hips all over his face. She had her hands on his head, calling out his name out in a low voice. Malachi stood up and observed Jasmine as she was taking deep breaths.

She got up and let her dress slide to the floor. Malachi looked in her eyes as she dropped to her knees, pulling his sweatpants and boxers down, showing his thick long manhood. She took him in her mouth slowly and deep till she could take her tongue and lick the bottom of his manhood where his balls were. She looked him in his eyes as she pulled him out slowly, rotating her hands all over his dick as she was sucking the head. She started licking up and down his dick, prompting Malachi to take deep breaths. He looked at her and picked her up off the floor, placing her on the bed doggy style..

He placed his hands on her ass as he slid inside of her, making her moan loud as he felt the back of her pussy. Jasmine had her legs on his thighs as he was taking deep strokes inside of her. With her ass in the air, she laid her head on his arm, biting down on her lip as his arms wrapped around her waist. Jasmine was trying to throw it back, but he was too big for her. Malachi loved the way her ass looked as he was sliding in and out of her. Pulling himself out of her, he laid on the bed as she climbed on top of him, riding him from the back. Malachi felt her wet tight box going up and down on him as his eyes were closed, smacking her ass twice as she was bouncing on him. He couldn't take it no more. Flipping her over and placing her legs on his shoulders, he started pounding into her hard and long until he unloaded his seed deep inside of her box. He then looked at her and kissed her lips as she was breathing hard, staring up at him as he was on top of her.

***

"How we looking out here, Detective Clark?"

Detective Clark looked at his partner as he smoked his cigarette.

"Someone took Pat and three of his men out last night. Pat was a high roller and the way it looks out here, whoever did this wasn't playing. They had a point to prove. We have M-16 shells, Mossberg shells, and Mac-11 shells. This was an assassination."

"You think someone is making a move on his turf?"

"I don't know, but if they are pulling up like this, we need to hurry up and get these bad guys off the street because they are not playing around. Looking at Pat over there, I think he pissed the wrong motherfucker off. Come on, Mark... it's time for us to do some investigation work to see who is carrying the guns that match these shells."

Chapter 12

Stacy walked the floor, watching all the females as they were working the tables, knowing everyone had their own story to tell. It's been two weeks since she had been left there. She had her freedom to walk around how she wanted to, eat what she wanted to when she wanted to, and people waited on her hand and foot. Kimberly told her some of the females had migrated there and this was a better life than what they had. Malachi had them all in their own little home on the farm. No one was a slave. They all made money to send home to their loved ones. How Malachi ran his cartel was different. If you fucked up, you died or for some females, he wouldn't kill them, he would put them in the Diamond Playhouse for punishment. You had to stay there for a year. Other cartels would beat you unconscious like a dog and you were a slave against your own will, eating food she wouldn't feed a dog in here. They made their own food, laughed, and joked, but they knew the rules. Rules were rules and that went for everyone, no exception. Within two weeks she was there, she counted up a thousand kilos of cocaine and had them ready to ship out. Kareem brought her first payment. She was lost for words when she seen the $50,000 dollars for the month. Every 15th of every month was a payday. She walked back to her office and sat behind her desk. When her office door opened, Kareem was standing there looking at her.

***

Jasmine laid her head on Malachi's chest and her arm was laying over his stomach as they laid in the bed together.

"Malachi, Manny told me that this week there's a big horse race at the track downtown and his champion horse is racing. He asked me if I would go to the race with him."

Malachi had his hand on Jasmine's head and was threading his fingers in her hair looking at her.

"Tell him yeah, you will go with him. This might be the perfect time to grab him. With you being there, he might not have all the security detail with him, maybe two at the most."

"I'll tell him. He said if I agree to go with him, meet him at the restaurant tonight at 8pm."

Malachi nodded and kissed Jasmine's forehead. She looked up at him and started kissing his neck softly as he wrapped his arm around her back, breathing softly in her ear as he felt her wetness sheath him as he sank into her depths.

***

"Stacy, you been with us for the last few weeks. You are a part of the cartel now. You know how deep our sources run. It's time you go show your face so the NYPD will drop this missing person case file on you. You will be brought back to New York City. Go see your mother and whoever else you need to see. Your career with *Wake Up New York* is over. They already replaced you. Your career is here with us now. In four days, your phone will ring. Pick it up and someone will meet you to pick you back up."

"What about the police? You don't think they will come asking me questions?"

"That's already been taken care of."

Kareem handed her some papers along with her cell phone before she dropped in the cab.

"What's this?"

"Receipts saying you were at a private range. It was a 60 day retreat. There are no loose strings. Everything is airtight."

Stacy nodded as she looked at the papers in her hand.

"Come on... there is one more thing we have to do before you leave."

Kareem walked Stacy to the burning room where they disposed of all evidence. She looked at him as he pulled the red hot iron brand out of the flames with the symbol of a broken diamond. Across the diamond it said "BDC" in cursive.

"Everyone in the cartel gets branded. Where do you want your stamp at?"

Stacy looked at Kareem and lifted her shirt up, showing her six pack abs.

"My side."

Kareem nodded and placed the hot iron on her flesh. Stacy let out a cry as he branded her. Kareem pulled the iron off her and handed her a stick of butter.

"Put this on there. You will be just fine. Come on, your ride is waiting on you."

Stacy nodded and walked off holding her side.

***

"Manny, do you have a second? There is something you need to know."

Manny looked at Cruise as he held an envelope in his hand while standing next to the living room table.

"Cruise, tell me what is so important you stopped me from watching my dog race when my pick number 12 is in the lead?"

"The female you were with the other night at the restaurant, she wasn't at the restaurant alone. Look, you see this guy in the picture. He was up on the second level. We think he was keeping an eye on her and look at this picture. This is them again together."

Manny was holding the pictures in his hand. He crumpled them and threw them on the floor.

"Find out where this bitch is at and let me know. I want to know who is this *puta* she is with. She got me feeling like a *pendejo*. I'm personally going to kill her."

"I have a guy who know where they are already."

"Good, take care of it." Manny walked off in a state of rage.

Cruise got three men and walked out the house to the Range Rover.

***

Malachi was standing in the penthouse looking out the window smoking a cigar. Jasmine walked up behind him.

"What's on your mind?"

"Getting this over with so we can get back to New York."

He stopped talking when he spotted a familiar black Range Rover pulling up outside the five star hotel and three Spanish men walking in. He remembered one of them from the restaurant the other night standing next to Manny.

"Jasmine, strap up. We have visitors and I don't think they here to talk." Malachi put the silencer on his gun and stood behind the door. Jasmine was standing by the window. When they strolled in the room, Cruise and three men walked in with guns out. Malachi came up from behind the door, shooting all three men in the back of the head, dropping them. When Cruise turned around, Malachi had a gun pointed at his head. Jasmine walked up to him, pointing her gun at him.

"Fuck up and die. Now drop the fucking gun."

Jasmine took the gun out of his hand and Cruise shook his head. Malachi walked up to him and put a chair in front of him.

"Yeah, you fucking up now. It's time to talk or you can lay next to the dead motherfuckers. Jasmine, in the next room, there's a black duffel bag on the floor. Go get it and bring it to me. As for you, you can sit down, or I can clap your ass and you can lay down. If you lay down, you ain't getting the fuck back up."

Cruise looked at Malachi and sat in the chair, not saying a word.

"Good fucking choice." Malachi said.

Jasmine brought the black duffel bag and placed it on the floor next to Malachi.

Chapter 13

"Shady, how we looking back there with that Baby Love?"

Shady placed the stack of money he had in his hand on the table as he looked at Cordial.

"This shit is bananas. Since that thunderstorm when Pat and them niggas got wet up, we pulling in twice the amount. This is 2.5 on the table right here, dog."

Cordial smiled as he pulled his cigar, looking at all the money on the table.

"When it rains, it pours. Baby boy bagged the bread up in stacks of a hundred grand. I'm about to hit Kareem up and tell him we need a pickup and drop off."

"Sayless, I'ma handle this cake and tap your line when it's bagged and tagged."

"Copy that."

Cordial walked off. He pulled his phone out and called Kareem. After a few rings he picked up.

"Cordial, talk to me."

"We ready for a pickup and drop off. We pulling in twice the amount since we had to rock-a-bye them fools."

Kareem pulled out his cigs as he watched Stacy's car as it pulled out from the farm.

"Can y'all hold the spot down for another 24 hours before I pull up?"

"Yeah."

"Cool. I'll see you then."

Kareem hung up the phone and walked to the shipping room. He waved Kimberly over to him.

"Yes, Kareem."

"Put 20 kilos together. Have them ready in an hour."

"Yes sir."

Kareem nodded and walked out of the room.

***

"Loyalty comes with a price. That price could be money or death, even prison. For your men right here, it was death, but the life we live is a game. Anybody can be removed off the board at a drop of a dime. The question is where does your loyalty stand?"

Malachi knelt down in front of Cruise and placed his gun up under his chin as Cruise was tied down to the chair with duct tape as he looked in his eyes.

"The man you devoted yourself to is a rat. We both know he's working for the FBI. He's an informant and that's who you stand next to, ready to die for. Give your life up for."

"Some of us didn't choose this life. We were forced into it. I don't speak on things because I like my tongue in my mouth. Some of us don't have a choice. I made my way up the ladder by not having a heart, by seeing it and not seeing it, hearing it and not hearing it. I know the stone I'm cut from."

Malachi walked to the table and picked up his cigar and relit it.

"How about I give you a choice today? Cruise, I know you are his second in command. I wash your hands, you wash mine. I don't want your blood on my hands. The only person I have an eye on is Manny. Nobody else's blood needs to be spilled. Help me get the man I have my eye on and you take his place leading the cartel, or you could die here today, right now. Either way, Manny is coming with me dead or alive, so make a choice here and now."

"If your plan backfires on me, your bullet won't mean shit to what Manny's cartel will do to me. Your bullet right now is an act of grace from Santa Maria."

"So, we have to make sure it doesn't backfire then. All I need you to do is tell me how to get to him when he is alone. When you do that, I will get him, and you're set free. These dead bodies right here will tell a story that you went out with a fight and shit just went bad."

Cruise took a deep breath.

"If you fuck me, I swear on Santa Maria, death can't keep me from you."

"You have my word, Cruise."

"From 6pm to 8pm, Manny prays to Santa Maria. No one is there with him. The house is empty. This is a everyday occurrence."

"Where do the guards go?"

"In town to eat."

Malachi nodded.

"Where in the house does he pray at?"

"Downstairs in the den."

Malachi looked at Jasmine then back at Cruise. He checked the time on his watch. It was 4:30pm.

"Jasmine, stay here with him. I'm going to get Manny. If you don't hear from me by 9pm, kill him."

"Malachi, come back to me."

"I will."

Malachi grabbed his coat and car keys as he walked out the door. He pulled his phone out and called Jason. After a few rings, Jason picked up.

***

Stacy stepped out of the car in Brooklyn and looked around. Before she could take two steps, someone called her name. She turned around and looked at one of her old co-workers as she walked up to Stacy, giving her a hug.

"Oh my God, Stacy! Where you been? There's been rumors that you were kidnapped by the cartel. Everyone's been worried sick over you."

"No, I been having some personal issues. I turned my phone off and went to a 60 day healing retreat."

"I'm so glad the rumors are not true."

Stacy let out a light laugh.

"Where did this rumor come from?"

"After you went missing, right after the interview with Captain Fuller, the rumors started."

"Whoa, I'm okay. Thanks for your concern, but I have to go see my mother Kiri, but it was good seeing you."

"You too, Stacy. Are you coming back to the station?"

"I don't know yet. Let me think about it. Take care, ok."

Stacy didn't say anything else, she just walked off, knowing her old life was dead. She was a part of one of the deadliest cartels now, if she had to wear their stamp, she was going to be the baddest and most deadliest bitch there. She had something to prove. Stacy Hall was dead, and Nicki Guns was alive now, and it was death before dishonor with The Black Diamond Cartel.

***

Malachi looked around the mansion as he walked along the walls with his gun out quietly. The mansion was empty besides Malachi and Jason's two men with him. As they were walking down the stairs, Malachi put his hand up to stop Jason's men from moving. Malachi was looking at Manny on his knees praying to Santa Maria in a dimly lighted room. The room was surrounded with candles. All of them were lit. Beads were hanging from the ceiling and candles surrounded the statue of Santa Maria. As Manny prayed to her, Malachi and Jason's men strode into the room. Manny didn't even know they were there. Malachi nodded to Jason's men. One of them walked up to Manny and smacked him in the back of the head with the gun, knocking him out cold.

"Grab him. Let's get the hell out of here before his security team comes back," Malachi ordered.

Then he walked out with Jason's men back to the truck. He looked around the property one more time before getting in the truck and drove off.

Chapter 14

Captain Fuller hung up the phone and looked at Agent Dawn. Captain Fuller got up and grabbed his coat from the back of the chair.

"Agent Dawn, you won't believe this. I just got a call saying Stacy Hall is at the tv station she used to work at."

"You have to be fucking kidding me? Let's go hear the story behind her disappearance."

When Captain Fuller and FBI Agent Dawn were getting out of the car in front of the tv station, Stacy Hall was walking out the doors to the station with a small box in her hands. She ran right into the both of them.

"Stacy Hall, you had a lot of people worried about you," Captain Fuller said as he and Agent Dawn approached her.

"Trust me, I know. I'm hearing the rumors about how I was kidnapped by the cartel. I just told my boss there was no truth to that at all."

Agent Dawn surveyed her and asked her, "If you don't mind me asking, where were you the last two months?"

"I was on a healing retreat. I was dealing with some personal problems, so I needed some time alone."

Captain Fuller and Agent Dawn exchanged glances when she said that.

"Where was the retreat at?"

Stacy placed the box down on the ground and reached into her purse and pulled out a receipt and brochure.

"It was in the Poconos, Agent Dawn."

Agent Dawn viewed the receipt and brochure and handed it to Captain Fuller. Captain Fuller inspected it and passed it back to Stacy.

"Stacy, since you been gone, four more females have been reported missing. Do you think we can air this on the tv station and pictures of these girls so we can try to crack down on this cartel?"

"Captain Fuller, I no longer work here. You'd have to go in and talk to them inside. I just came to get my belongings as you can see. Now if you don't mind, I have to get going, officers."

Both scrutinized Stacy as she walked off.

"Fuller, I don't believe a word she just said. I don't care about no receipt or brochure. She's lying."

"Yeah, I get that same feeling, Dawn."

Both men got back in the car and drove off.

***

Jasmine looked at the time on the wall clock. It was 8:55pm. She walked to the table and picked her cell phone up and peeked at it then at Cruise tied down to the chair. Still, she picked up her gun and cocked it back and walked to Cruise.

"If Malachi don't call in the next five minutes, you going to hear that pop."

Cruise didn't respond. He just looked at her. Jasmine looked at the time again. It read 8:59pm. Jasmine pointed the gun at Cruise's head.

"I think it's time you say your prayers to Santa Maria."

Right before she was about to pull the trigger, her phone went off. Seeing it was Malachi calling her, she picked up the phone to the sound of Malachi's voice.

"We good, everything went beautiful. I'll be there in 20 minutes. Keep him tied down."

Jasmine hung up the phone.

"I guess your prayer worked. Malachi will be here in a few then you are a free man."

***

Kareem was in the backseat of the car headed to New Jersey when Stacy called him. He put the cigar he was smoking in the ashtray and answered the phone.

"You ready to come back already."

"No, I was calling because I ran into both Captain Fuller and an FBI agent. I showed them the receipt and brochure. Then they started talking about four more females that been kidnapped. I told them I had to go and walked off."

Kareem just nodded while listening to Stacy.

"You did good. Just stay away from them. I'll send someone to pick you up tomorrow."

"I'll call you after 12pm."

"I'll be waiting on your call." Kareem hung up the phone and called Malachi. After a few seconds Malachi picked up.

"Talk to me. Is everything alright?"

"Yeah, things are good with Stacy. I stamped her like you said, but she just told me that Captain Fuller and an FBI agent are asking her questions about the four females that been kidnapped."

Malachi looked out the window of the Maybach he was riding in on the way to Mexico to see Blanka.

"You know what? If they want them that bad kill them and hang them outside across the street tonight from Captain Fuller's office window where he can see them in the morning. Maybe then he will get the picture of who he's dealing with. Bring Stacy with you. It's time to break her in the right way."

"I'll take care of that now."

"Good. I should be back in the next two or three days. I'll see you then."

"Copy."

Malachi hung up the phone and placed his finger on his chin as he went into deep thought. The truth about Mrs. Blanka's son and grandson was about to come to the light. And who knows what the blowback was going to be once it did.

Chapter 15

Blanka walked outside where his mother was. He watched as she placed two roses down next to her son's and grandson's headstones that she personally picked from her garden. Blanka walked up behind his mother and placed his hand on her shoulder. Without looking back at him, she placed her hand on top of his.

"Mama, I know you mourn deeply for our loved ones."

"I do, Blanka, but Santa Maria answered my prayers. Soon, Manny's bones will be lying next to our children in this cold wet grave."

"What do you mean, Mama?"

Blanka's mother turned around and faced him, looking deep into his eyes.

"Malachi has Manny. He will be here shortly with him, then I will kill him personally over what he took from us."

"That's good news. Let me go wait for Malachi so I can take him to the back when he arrives."

"Go ahead. I'm going to spend more time here, my child."

Blanka kissed his mother's hand and walked off.

***

Malachi looked at Jasmine as she was lost in her thoughts. He knew something was on her mind. Jasmine had never been to Blanka's house before, but he wanted to know what she was thinking.

"Jasmine, what's on your mind?"

"We both know that Blanka had his hands in his brother and son's deaths. We have the man who called the hit but wasn't responsible for their murder. Manny's shooters missed, but Blanka's didn't. Blanka wanted you to bring him back dead. His mother wanted you to bring him back alive. How is this going to play out when the truth comes out?"

"Blanka's mother is the head of the cartel. My oath is with her, not Blanka. Before I let Blanka kill him, his mother and wife will know the truth, and this will give us our freedom from their cartel. Today, Blanka will see loyalty comes with a price. Just make sure you have one in the head. Move when I say move. Shoot when I shoot."

"Always, Malachi. I will follow your lead."

Malachi nodded and lit his cigar, already knowing how this might play out.

***

Blanka was out front when Malachi's car pulled up. Blanka had five of his guards with him standing side by side. Angie was in the upstairs window looking down at everything. Blanka never moved from where he was. Malachi's driver opened up the back door for Malachi and Jasmine to get out. Then he walked to the trunk of the car and opened it. He put a brown bag over Manny's head and took him by the arm and walked him towards Blanka. Jasmine looked around at the big mansion and the guards standing around with assault rifles in their hands. Blanka waved his hand for Malachi to follow him. They all walked to the back far end of the yard to a garage. Malachi placed Manny in a chair that was there and took the bag off his head. As they tied him down, Manny looked around at everyone. He could not talk because he had duct tape over his mouth. Blanka walked up to Malachi.

"Malachi, I gave you a direct order to kill this man, not to bring him back here alive."

Jasmine glanced around at the guards holding the assault rifles before looking at Malachi.

"I know what you said to me. I got your messages, Blanka, but my blood oath is with your mother. She wants him alive, so your direct order means nothing to me."

Blanka smiled and nodded at one of the guards.

"You kill Manny now."

Malachi stepped in front of him and pulled his gun out, putting the bead in the center of the other man's forehead.

"You kill him. I kill you."

Blanka pulled his gun out and pointed it at Malachi. Jasmine pulled her gun out and had the barrel pointed at Blanka's head. All the guards had their guns pointed at Jasmine and Malachi.

"Malachi, you are signing your own death warrant here."

"Then let that be the reason that my blood spills. I am a man who fears no one."

Blanka took a deep breath. That's when his mother and wife walked into the garage. Blanka's mother peered at Jasmine and Malachi.

"Malachi, you pull a gun on my *only child* at *my house* after all we've done for you?"

"Mrs. Blanka, your son tried to kill this man because he didn't want his dark secret to come out before you got here."

Mrs. Blanka eyeballed Blanka, looking a little lost over what Malachi said.

"Blanka, what is he talking about?"

"Nothing, this *puta* is lying, Mama."

"Am I? Blanka, tell your mother the truth. Why is her oldest son dead and your wife's son as well?"

Malachi stared at Angie when he said that.

"Blanka, tell me it's *not* true… that you knew *the truth* all this time and never told me. Tell me it's not true," his mom pleaded.

Blanka just glared at Malachi, not paying no attention to his mother.

"Mrs. Blanka, I'll tell y'all the deadliest truth about y'all sons' murders."

Angie walked up to Malachi. "Malachi, please don't tell me Blanka has their blood on his hands."

"Mrs. Blanka, Angie, over a year ago, Blanka called a hit on Keko and had him killed. Angie, your son was there with Keko. Blanka didn't know so when they shot up Keko's car, they not only killed him but your son too."

"Mama, he's lying."

"So, why did you want him brought back dead? Because you didn't want Manny to tell the truth. Mrs. Blanka, look at this."

Malachi never took his eyes off of Blanka as he pointed his gun at him. He reached into his pocket and pulled out his cell phone and handed it to Mrs. Blanka.

"Read the text message your son sent me."

She took the phone and viewed the message then eyed Blanka.

"Blanka, why? Why did you do this?"

Angie couldn't believe what she was hearing as she looked at her husband, the man who murdered their son, their only child in cold blood.

"Mama, he was going to bring the family down. I had to make a hard decision and I chose the cartel, Mama."

Mrs. Blanka walked up to her son and kissed him on the cheek, then over to Malachi and took her hand and lowered his arm. As she looked into Malachi's eyes, taking his gun from him, a tear dropped from her eye. Turning around, she shot Blanka dead in the neck. His body hit the ground, causing him to drop his gun. She staggered up to Angie and handed her the gun. Angie pointed it at Blanka's head and fired two rounds, killing him quickly. Mrs. Blanka walked up to Malachi and kissed him on the cheek.

"Manny never killed my child, Malachi?"

"No, Mrs. Blanka. He tried and missed. Not even 10 minutes later, Blanka had his men kill him."

Mrs. Blanka scrutinized Blanka's personal guard before walking up to him.

"You were there. You have my son's and grandson's blood on your hands."

"Mrs. Blanka, I did what I was told by Blanka. I didn't know it was your son's or Angie's son."

"But you never said *nothing* when you *did know*... their blood is on your hands too."

He looked around and stepped back, pointing the gun at Mrs. Blanka. Jasmine seen the look in his eyes. He was ready to die, but not alone. She fired two shots at him, hitting him in the arm and shoulder, dropping him. Malachi ran and kicked him in the face and picked up his gun. Mrs. Blanka looked at Jasmine then the guard.

"Don't kill him. I want him alive, Malachi.

"What about Manny?"

Mrs. Blanka pulled a knife out of her pocket, moseyed up to Manny, and slit his throat from ear to ear, watching him bleed out as the blood dripped off her knife onto the ground.

"It is done." she slumped to the ground, revenge has certainly taken its toll.

Chapter 16

The streets were packed with people watching the scene. There were 20 plus officers walking around with yellow caution tape blocking people off. Two local news teams were running the story live. Captain Fuller couldn't believe what he was seeing. FBI Agent Dawn and Chief Ward drifted up to him as he examined the four females hanging by their necks across the street from his office window at a construction site.

"Somebody wanted you to know they got your message, Captain Fuller."

"I see this has become personal now. Their blood is on my hands. He killed them because I was looking for them, Chief Ward."

"Yeah, they had to bring them here last night. Do you know if they were dead or alive?"

Agent Dawn shook his head.

"No, Chief, they walked them in that construction site. The cause of death was hanging by the neck."

"Agent Dawn, the only person we talked to about the missing females was Stacy Hall. She told them we were looking for the four females and last night, they gave them to us. We need to find Stacy Hall now! She's not telling us what really happened."

Agent Dawn took a deep breath. "I've seen this before, Fuller. She was gorilla breed. The Stacy we are looking for now isn't the Stacy Hall that was kidnapped. The Stacy we are looking for is a part of the cartel now and if she is walking around like this, it means she has a stamp from someone high up in the organization."

Captain Fuller and Chief Ward gawked at Agent Dawn as she talked. Captain Fuller walked off. Chief Ward yelled out to him. "Where you going, Captain?"

"To find Stacy Hall."

"I'm going with him, Chief."

Chief Ward watched on as Agent Dawn ran behind Captain Fuller.

***

Kareem walked into the project with his four guards, observing everyone around the building as he walked up to Cordial's apartment door. He knocked two times before someone peeked out the peephole at him. He heard the locks on the door unlocking before the door opened. Kareem walked inside with his men up to Cordial and Shady. Two of the guards placed the duffle bags on the floor next to Cordial's feet.

"There's 20 kilos in these two duffle bags. I see the storm bring out a brighter day for us over here."

Shady bent down and opened the duffle bag up and smiled when he seen the kilos inside.

"Yeah, we are 100% over here right now. When is Malachi coming back?"

"Two or three days he said, but look, I have to go pick up Stacy, so let me get that bread so I can bounce."

"Sayless. I thought Stacy was with you last night."

"She was. She did her part. She had to take care of some other business, so I dropped her off in Brooklyn last night. Once I leave here, I'm going to pick her back up."

Shady walked up to Kareem and handed the duffle bags with the money inside to the guards that was with him.

"2.5 in both of them bags altogether, Kareem."

"Y'all niggas stay up. I'm out."

Shady dapped Kareem up before he walked out the apartment with his four guards.

***

"Malachi, you have been loyal to my cartel and my family. It's because of you I have peace in my heart now. Jasmine, you saved my life. I will never forget that. If there's anything I can do for you and Malachi, just let me know and it's done."

Malachi sauntered over to Mrs. Blanka and held her hand.

"Mrs. Blanka, I've been under your cartel for the last few years. Today, I'm asking you to set me free. I will still be loyal to you, but I want to be my own man governed by my own laws."

"Malachi, you are free, but you will always have ties with us. Promise me that today, right here, right now."

"I promise you that on the blood of my diamond."

Mrs. Blanka kissed Malachi on the cheek and took her thumb and wiped it off.

"Before you leave Malachi, there is one more thing I want to show you and Jasmine. Come with me."

Malachi and Jasmine walked to the back of the house where Mrs. Blanka had Manny's and Blanka's dead bodies laying in an open grave while Blanka's guard was beaten to an inch of his life with black and blue marks all over him, lying motionless on the ground.

"Malachi, death comes in threes. This man tried to take my life and he would've had it if it wasn't for you, Jasmine. Death will find him soon. I will not kill him. Jasmine, do you mind taking your foot and pushing him in the hole. He will be buried alive."

Jasmine walked up to him and placed her foot on his chest and shoulder, pushing his body in the grave. She then looked at the guards standing around before walking back and standing next to Malachi. Jasmine read the headstone. It said: *Loyalty comes with a price. Death comes in threes. Santa Maria sees it all.* Malachi kissed Mrs. Blanka's forehead and walked off with Jasmine, knowing he was a free man able to run his own cartel, but when Mrs. Blanka called, he must be ready to answer.

Chapter 17

"Today, we buried four of our brothers, three bodies and one in spirit. We are not going to fool ourselves. Today, Manny's body may not be here with us, but we know he's dead. He's been missing for a week now, kidnapped out of his own home. His blood was on the floor in front of Santa Maria as he prayed to her. We are at war. Let it be known we have $100,000 reward for any information leading to the person responsible for this. We will let it be known what happened when you fuck with Manny's cartel."

Cruise looked around at everyone standing, knowing he had a team of devoted loyal killers backing him up as the new head of the cartel.

***

Kareem walked up to Malachi smiling as he greeted him with open arms as Malachi stepped out of the car at the farm.

"Tell me, Kareem, how are things here since I been gone?"

"Cordial and Shady made it rain and a few people got wet up. Stacy broke the ice. I had her put that work in across the street from you know who. I stood there and watched her as she did it. She goes by the name Nicki Guns now."

Malachi smiled and pulled out two cigars and handed one to Kareem.

"Nicki Guns, where is she at now?" Malachi asked as he lit his cigar.

"She's in her office, going over the cocaine count this week."

Malachi nodded.

"I think I'ma go have a one on one talk with her. I'll be back in a few."

"I'll be out here if you need me."

"I already know."

Malachi wandered off. When he reached Stacy's door, he knocked two times before he heard her voice say, "Come in."

He opened the door and stared at her. Stacy got up and walked around her desk. Malachi gazed at the female who no longer looked like Stacy Hall from *Wake Up New York*, but the Nicki Guns with the Black Diamond Cartel. Stacy stood there looking like a real boss bitch with her dark red hair, light brown eyes, honey brown skin, and a body Beyonce would kill for. She wore a red tight leather dress that stopped at her kneecaps paired with red two inch open toe heels. Her toenails were painted white, the same as her fingernails. Malachi was lost for words while inspecting the dime piece standing in front of him with the diamond chain around her neck and with the red sleeve going from her hands to her elbow that matched her dress.

"Sit down and relax, Nicki, let's talk."

Nicki sat at the table right across from Malachi.

"Can I get you something to drink, Malachi… wine, water, or something stronger?"

"Yeah, get me and you something stronger."

Nicki got up and walked to the bar in her office as Malachi pulled out a cigar and lit it. Nicki walked backed to the table and handed Malachi a glass of gin on the rocks.

"Thank you."

"Do you know who I am?"

Nicki shook her head. "Yes, your name is Malachi. You are the head of The Black Diamond Cartel."

"Yes, I am. Any questions you want to ask me right here, right now is the time."

Malachi pulled on his cigar as he studied Nicki.

"You could've killed me for what I said on *Wake Up New York*, but you didn't. You put me in the Diamond Playhouse and then brought me here. Why am I still breathing and not at the Diamond Playhouse but here?"

"Nicki, you played with a double edge sword talking about the cartel. I could have had your body dumped in the East River, but death would have been an easy way out. I wanted you to see first-hand what those females go through from the way they lived to the fact that they don't have a say in what I tell them to do. They will fuck and suck dick until I tell them to stop. I wanted you to see what it was like to count, bag, and weigh up kilos of cocaine to see the farm and the workers on the farm. I wanted you to understand this *is* your life now. The stamp on your side wasn't enough. I needed blood on your hands as well. I wanted all the innocence you had purged. So, I had you kill four innocent females whose only crime was that a detective or captain and an FBI agent was asking questions about them. Everything you talked about from sex trafficking, drug trafficking, kidnapping, and murder, I had you do within 60 days. I had Kareem stamp you personally for me. That's why you are sitting here right now in your office."

Malachi took a sip of his gin on the rocks as he looked at Nicki.

"I made my bed and I'm laying in it, but you should know now, if this is the life I have to live, I'm the deadliest bad bitch in The Black Diamond Cartel. I promise you that."

"Good, because you have my stamp. There are only two rules I want you to live by. One, loyalty covers everything. Two, kill everything your enemies care about. Make them beg for mercy. Deny it until their last breath. That's how you prove your loyalty to me."

Nicki nodded and took her shot of gin.

"Now come on, it's time… we all have a meeting to go to. You need to meet the other four, Jasmine, Shady, Cordial, and B-More."

Malachi got up from the table and walked out the office with Nicki right behind him.

Chapter 18

"Detective Mark, I got your page. You wanted to see me?"

"Yeah, I think I found out who's behind Pat's murder."

Detective Clark took a seat in front of Detective Mark's desk.

"Let me hear this one, Mark."

"All I know right now is that they are from New York, and they are a few projects down from where Pat was working out of."

"Now, it's all coming together. They start moving weight, Pat's pockets were becoming light. Pat sends some of his guys to check them and some not so friendly words were said."

"Not only that, Clark, the body that was found in the bricks, that was one of Pat's guys name Rockma, who used to be off Patterson."

Detective Clark pointed his finger at Detective Mark as he bit his bottom lip.

"You know a few days before Pat's murder, dispatch got a 911 call saying there was a shootout in Diane Projects and two people were shot. When the blue and white got there, the place was empty."

"There you have it. Pat sends his shooters. One gets killed. Someone else gets shot. These guys from New York shoot back, killing Pat and three of his men. You know what, Clark? I bet if you check around in New York, call in a favor or two, a body might come up in the last week."

"While you do that, I'ma go see what I can find out about the shooting over there in Diane Projects."

"Sure, I'll keep you posted on what I find out."

"Likewise."

***

Malachi and Nicki walked into the back room in the greenhouse on the far end. When Malachi opened the door, all eyes were on him and Nicki. As they walked in the room, everyone who was sitting down stood up out of respect for Malachi. Malachi took his seat at the head of the table then everyone sat down behind him. Malachi didn't say a word to anybody. He pulled his cigar out and relit it. He looked at Kareem and nodded. Kareem stood up.

"In the time of your absence, we, or should I say Cordial and Shady, took over Diane Projects. The last count we got from over there was 2.5 million. They had to lay the murder game down, but they weren't the ones who drew first blood. The two officers that were asking questions about the four missing females, Nicki and I made sure that they found all four of them with a bird's eye view. The Diamond Playhouse is still running smooth. We just dropped three more females off there last night. All the kilos are accounted for, thanks to Nicki Guns."

Kareem sat down after giving his report.

"Thank you for that, Kareem. As of two days ago, we are our own cartel. Jasmine and I took care of a blood oath with Blanka's cartel that gave us our freedom. Cordial and Shady will continue the operation in New Jersey. Kareem, you and Jasmine have Brooklyn. B-More, you will be stationed here in upstate New York. I want everyone to keep in mind we are our own cartel now. So that means a lot of people might be coming after us. Not just the police and FBI, but other cartels… maybe even the mob. Y'all know the rules: One, loyalty that covers everything. Two, strength in the cartel means kill everything your enemies care about. Make them beg for mercy. Deny it until they take their last breath. Remember we are The Black Diamond Cartel and loyalty comes with a price."

***

Cruise was sitting at the table talking with one of the members from Bone's cartel when one of his workers walked up to him and told him something in his ear. Cruise looked at the man and grabbed him by the shirt and and then pulled him back down to him. Cruise told the man something back and let him go. Cruise looked at Bone's man and shook his head as he took a deep breath.

"I'm sorry but I have to take care of some very important business that just came to my attention. Will you let Bone know that I will make sure his shipment gets to him this week and thank you for your business?"

"I will let him know everything you said."

"Thank you." Cruise shook his hand as he got ready to walk out the office. Cruise looked over at his guard. "Come here."

When the guard walked up to Cruise, he pointed his finger in his face.

"Your people better not be wrong about this or it's your ass that's going to be on the line. Tell everyone get ready. We are about to take a ride to see Jason White."

Cruise took his hand and rubbed his chin as he started putting everything together. He walked outside and got into the black Range Rover. He cocked his gun back as he rode to Jason White's apple patch.

"When these trucks stop, we ain't doing no talking. Every motherfucker dies. Don't nobody touch Jason. He's mine!"

Nobody said a word. They just looked at him and nodded.

***

Jasmine didn't say a word as she looked out the window of the Maybach as she and Kareem were headed back to Brooklyn. Kareem lit his cigar and looked at Jasmine.

"Jasmine, what's that look on your face mean?"

"I have killed detectives for this cartel and people before we became a cartel. I've been shot at. I just came back from Mexico with having Blanka's men pointing assault rifles at me, ready to roll me. We killed Manny's men. I held the new head of the cartel in El Paso, Texas at gunpoint while he was tied down to a chair. I was *here* from the very start, and he is sending me back to Brooklyn while he's staying in upstate New York with Nicki. That's a spit in my fucking face."

"Jasmine, we all are living a nefarious lifestyle. It's what we committed to. You are a soldier who knows when to strike and when to lay back and observe. Malachi trust you with his life. That's why he took you with him to El Paso. He needs you right here in Brooklyn at Admiral Row Apartments. He knows what you are about. Already pulling dirty cops' tongues through their throats, your body count is real. You are a boss bitch riding around in a 2022 Genesis G70 2. OT Sedan. Remember this Jasmine, you are *the bitch* that took pictures of Detective Benloss's wife and kids then bodied the fool when he ran up on you in the elevator. We all have a part to play. Trust me, he has his reason for having you out here."

"Yeah, you right. I guess I was just in my bag that's all."

"I already know, trust me."

"So, tell me what went down with Nicki breaking the ice?"

"I ain't going to lie. That's a long story, but that bitch was ruthless that night."

***

Cruise looked around as his men shot down everything around them from the maids, men and female workers, dragging them outside and putting a bullet to their heads as he walked with his gun in his hand up to Jason White. His men had him tied up to a tree, beaten badly. Cruise walked up to him and tapped him twice on the cheek with his open palm.

"You know it took me some time to put it all together, Jason, but I did. It was *you* setting everything up from the start. The meeting at Jimmy's restaurant with Manny. That meeting was just so whoever kidnapped him could see who he was and how he moved. Then when I called you about the shipment, you told me you changed your mind on the 400 units. Jason… Jason… you fucked up now. Look at you. A lot of your people are dead, and here you are tied down to a tree. You are going to tell me what I want to know or it is going to be a very slow and painful death for you."

Jason knew he was going to die. Malachi kept his word with him. He was more than a friend, but an honest and fair businessman. Loyalty was the only thing that came to his mind at that point in time.

"I don't know what the fuck you are talking about. If Manny is dead, it's the bed *he* made for himself. Karma is a bitch and she is all too happy to fuck him in it." Jason said with short breaths.

Cruise searched around before his eyes saw a chainsaw on the ground. He walked over to it and picked it up. He smiled and looked at Jason.

"You know what the chainsaw's original name was, Jason? The original name was called the *Bone Cutter*. Let's put that name to the test. What you say?"

Cruise pulled the cord, bringing the chainsaw to life, walking up to Jason.

"You ain't got to tell me what I want to know, but when the motherfucker sees what I have done to you, they going to get the picture of who the fuck we are and Jason, this is going to hurt you a lot more than it is gonna hurt me."

Cruise strode up to Jason, slamming the chainsaw blade on Jason's shoulder blade. Jason yelled out in pain as blood flew everywhere as Cruise cut through his bone, killing him. Cruise dropped the chainsaw on the ground and looked at his men.

"Burn the house down and everything around it. Whoever killed Manny is going to get the picture, we ain't playing."

Cruise took a rag out his back pocket and wiped the blood off his face as he walked back to the Range Rover.

Chapter 19

District Attorney Cox walked into Captain Fuller's office smiling like the cat who ate the canary.

"Cox, tell me the deal with your informant is a go."

District Attorney Cox showed Captain Fuller the papers signed off by the mayor on the deal.

"That's the best news I saw all day, so we need to go see Cox."

"We need to take a trip to California and El Paso, Texas and have a few words with a Jason White. That's going to be the path that leads us to Malachi Williams."

"Well, you know what? It's time for us to go take that plane ride. Let's go run this by the chief. He's in the office talking to Agent Dawn."

"After you."

Both men walked to Chief Ward's office. Captain Fuller knocked two times before he heard the chief say, *"come in."* When they opened the door Chief Ward and Agent Dawn were sitting down talking. Both men looked at them when they walked in.

"Now lookee what we have here, District Attorney Cox and Captain Fuller walking into my office side by side with some papers in their hands. This has got to be good. Tell me what we got?"

"We have a name, Jason White, and he's the path to Malachi Williams. We have the papers here and the deal is signed off by the mayor. Everything is a go, sir."

"Wait, run that name by me again, Fuller."

"Jason White."

Agent Dawn took a deep breath, prompting everyone to turn their attention to him.

"What is the bullshit that you are about to drop on our parade, Dawn?" Chief Ward asked him expectantly.

"Jason White was brutally murdered three days ago at his apple range in El Paso, Texas. They tied him to a tree and cut him open with a chainsaw from his shoulder across his chest. Then burned down his range and everything around it."

Captain Fuller dropped the papers on Chief Ward's desk and shook his head as he threw his hands in the air.

"We just can't get a fucking break."

Captain Fuller walked out of Chief Ward's office seething.

"Chief Ward, how is it that District Attorney Cox can find out who Malachi Williams' connect is, and not even three days after he gets the deal signed, Jason White turns up dead?"

"What, you think there's a mole somewhere, Agent Dawn?"

"I don't know, but we need to get to the bottom of this shit *now*."

"I agree. We all need to make some phone calls now."

DA Cox and Agent Dawn got up and walked out of the chief's office as Chief Ward picked up the phone and called out.

***

Malachi sat in his office questioning himself. Should he have killed Cruise when he had the chance? He always was a man who honored his word. He let Cruise live and Cruise killed Jason in a horrible way. With his own cartel behind him, Malachi knew he was untouchable and soon to be unstoppable. He knew Cruise had to be behind the scene. They couldn't stop what they couldn't see. As long as everyone played their part, they were going to take over more than the east coast. Jason's dead, Blanka's dead, and Manny's dead. The fact that Manny was dead was behind breaking the number one rule– he believed the feds and was in bed with them. Blanka broke the rules too— disloyalty to the family. It not only cost him his life, but his brother's and son's too. Jason broke one of the biggest rules as well— becoming too comfortable in this life we live. Mrs. Blanka was right when she said, "Death comes in threes." They all were loyal to themselves and like the saying goes, "loyalty comes with a price," and death was their price, and she collected on it. He questioned his recent actions. Did he break a deadly rule by letting Cruise live? And by doing so did he show weakness on his part?

Chapter 20

One year later

Malachi looked out the window as the Maybach pulled up in front of Admiral Row Apartments. He watched the door open as Nicki stepped out looking like a runway model walking into the apartments. He ambled to his desk and sat behind it as he lit his cigar while waiting for her to walk into his office. He looked up as his office door opened and Nicki walked in. Standing, Malachi strolled to the front of his desk as she walked up to him, hugging him and kissing him on both cheeks.

"Have a seat, Nicki, and tell me what brings you all the way from upstate New York down here to Brooklyn?"

Nicki sat down in front of Malachi's desk as he sat behind it.

"I have been loyal, honest, and devoted to the cartel over the last year and a half. Everyone is doing their own thing and still putting the cartel first."

Malachi listened to Nicki quietly as she continued.

"I want to do something. I know a lot of people who play with their noses from *Wake Up New York.* I just don't want to stay upstate New York. I want to make my own moves like everyone else and I want your blessing on this."

Malachi placed his cigar in the ashtray on his desk and rubbed his chin thoughtful as he looked at Nicki.

"You came here today asking me for a pass. You have been honest, devoted, and loyal to the cartel. If I do this, *nothing* will come free for you. You will pay dues to the cartel. 25% every month. Every unit will cost you $16,000. You will still have to continue operations in upstate New York. That being said, I'ma give you your pass, but this ain't no friendly push out the nest. Nothing you do better not blow back on The Black Diamond Cartel. No one you work with will know of me or my existence, or any of my business dealings with you. I will give you a three month leave of absence to get your affairs in order. I see the look in your eyes. You are asking yourself, *'Why am I doing this to you and not Jasmine, Shady, Kareem, or B-More, even Cordial? And why am I being so hard on you and not them?'* Let me answer your question for you."

Malachi got up and walked from behind his desk up to Nicki. She stood up as he held her hand and looked into her eyes.

"Because you are *my* stamp. Nothing ever came easy to me. Now look where I stand. No one has my signature stamp but *you* on your side. I personally had that made for you. Everyone else just has the broken diamond."

Nicki looked in Malachi's eyes, "Malachi, I promise I will give my all to you. I won't let you down. I will risk my life for you."

"I know, Nicki." Malachi took his hand and placed it under her chin and kissed her lips. He then looked deep into her eyes. "That kiss was a seal of our trust between us. Now I believe you have some work to do."

Nicki nodded and walked off. Malachi knew Nicki was going to be his bottom bitch and she was going to be the one down to do what no one else could else could do in his cartel. Not because of her loyalty or devotion, but the fire that burned bright in her eyes; she had something to prove to herself.

***

Cordial walked up to Detective Clark and handed him a paper bag as he stood behind the garbage dumpster in the alley.

"You know, a year ago, you walked in Diane Projects asking questions about a murder. I killed all that line of questioning off and started paying you and Detective Mark

The Black Diamond Cartel 2

$10,000 a piece so the questions would simply go away. Here I am a year later still paying you. My point is this shit is getting old, Detective Clark."

"Old to you, still new to me."

"Well, if you are going to be pulling up about this bread, y'all niggas are going to go on payroll. Fuck all this free shit."

Detective Clark walked up to Cordial. "So, what you saying?"

"Nigga, this payday shit is over unless y'all ready to work for me now."

"Y'all New York niggas got some balls I'll give you that. I'll see you next month, Cordial, and have my bread or next our next conversation won't be so friendly."

Cordial gawked at Detective Clark as he walked off, knowing bodying a detective wasn't the smart move right now. Badge or no badge, he wasn't going out like no chump. Detective Clark would be laying in a pool of blood first with a slug in his chest, trying to catch his breath before he sold out like a bitch to a pig with a badge.

Chapter 21

Nicki's car pulled up in front of Whitney Plaza. Her driver stepped out of the car and opened her door for her to get out. Nicki stepped out the car looking like a boss bitch. Everything she had on was Prada. She looked at her driver.

"I'll be out in a few. Don't go too far."

She turned away from him and walked inside the plaza, right up the front counter.

"I need to speak to your manager. Is he around?"

"Yes, I will get him. Hold on one second please."

"Sure, I'll be right here when you get back."

Within two minutes, the manager of the plaza walked up to Nicki on the other side of the counter.

"Good afternoon. My name is Alex Goodman. I'm the manager here. How may I help you?"

"Good afternoon, Mr. Goodman. My name is Stacy Hall and I'm looking to rent one of your penthouse suites."

"Stacy Hall, I used to watch you on *Wake Up New York* all the time. Please come into my office and we'll go over some options."

"Please lead the way."

Stacy followed him to his office right up to his desk.

"Please have a seat. Now we have one left. It's a 3 bedroom, two bathroom, a living room, den, and kitchen. It's 2600 square feet and the unit is $4,300 a month with a deposit of $12,000 down. That will cover two months' rent and your security deposit. Here is a brochure of the unit."

Stacy looked at the brochure and smiled.

"If I want my residence here to be private, would that be a problem?"

"No, that would not be a problem at all."

"Good, I'll take it then."

Stacy opened her Prada bag and pulled out $20,000 dollars and placed it on Mr. Goodman's desk.

"This is $20,000 dollars. It should cover four months' rent and my security deposit."

"Yes, it will. Let me just get the paperwork ready for you."

"I'm on your time, Mr. Goodman."

Stacy wanted everything she did to be private. She was going to run her operation out of Manhattan. She needed some hustlers and gorillas in the streets moving her product. With the money she saved up, she got herself 20 kilos of cocaine to start with. She had a personal driver taking her around in her Maybach. She knew not to shit where she resided, so she had her driver take her to the east side of Harlem to 137th on down. She was going to be the queen of Harlem and that's where she was going to start her thumping grounds.

***

Malachi walked into his office to hear Mariah Carey singing in the background, "*I give my all to you.*" He looked around to see Jasmine walking up to him with just a red lace bra and G-string on with 2 inch open-toe heels. Her hair was pulled back. Malachi licked his lips as she ambled up to him, kissing on the side of his neck. He took two steps back and closed and locked his office door. He picked Jasmine up and carried her to his desk, pulling his pants and boxers down as he kissed her. Jasmine wrapped her legs around his back as his manhood slid into her honey pot. Jasmine let out a light moan as Malachi held her and sucked on her neck, smelling her sweet perfume. He stopped and looked into her beautiful eyes. In that moment he knew he was falling in love with her.

"Malachi, I love you, and I hope it ain't wrong to love you because I give my all for you."

Malachi was lost when Jasmine said that. He had a flashback of him putting his finger on Nicki's chin and kissing her after she told him the same thing. Jasmine took her hands and placed them on his face, kissing him as she looked in his eyes. Malachi pulled his face back.

"Jasmine?"

"Yes."

"I love you, too." Malachi admitted as he started kissing her again.

Chapter 22

Captain Fuller picked up his cup of coffee and walked into the investigation room. He hadn't been there in the last few months. He walked up to the bulletin board and looked at everyone who was under investigation. There were pictures of mafia families, gangs, and the old picture they had of Malachi and pictures of his crew. He stopped when he seen the picture of Stacy Hall, not in the pictures of Malachi's crew, but a whole other part of the bulletin board by herself getting out of the Maybach with a mink coat on. She had bodyguards with her, walking on each side of her with diamond chains and earrings.

"You have to be fucking kidding me. Hey you, come here."

The officer walked up to Captain Fuller.

"Whose investigation is this? Who's investigating her?"

"No one. Those pictures got sent over from the 54th police station in Harlem. They are part of the station to station crime stoppers the mayor started last year. All we know is that they call her Nicki Guns, nothing else. They know she's *somebody*, but they don't have nothing on her yet."

Captain Fuller walked out the investigation room, phone in hand. He called FBI Agent Dawn. After a few seconds Agent Dawn picked up.

"Agent Dawn speaking."

"Dawn, it is Fuller. You got a few seconds. We need to talk."

"Sure, I ain't doing nothing. What's up?"

"I just left the investigation room, and we have pictures of Stacy Hall on the board looking like a real boss bitch, mink coat, Maybach, and bodyguards walking on the east side of Harlem."

"You know what, Fuller? We had a briefing about a female in Harlem riding around in a Maybach. Let me turn on my computer. I had the pictures sent to my e-mail a week ago. I just have been so busy on the fifteen dead females in the box truck and the four females that were hanging from the building. So much is going on, I haven't even looked into the case file. Ok, I'm opening up the email now."

Agent Dawn cursed as he pulled up the pictures of Stacy Hall.

"Yeah, she's doing something, Fuller."

"How does she go from Wake Up New York to this, Dawn?"

"I don't know, but I think we need to find out."

"That's the same thing I was thinking."

"Let me make some calls and I'll call you back, Fuller."

"I'll be waiting to hear from you."

Captain Fuller hung up the phone and looked out the window of his office to where the females were hung—they were getting close to figuring this whole tangled web of deception out, he could feel it in his bones.

***

Malachi was smoking a cigar when Kareem walked into his office.

"How we looking out there, Kareem?"

Kareem strolled to the bar and poured himself a glass of gin and juice. Then he walked over to Malachi.

"All the numbers are good. As I was going over the books, I noticed for the last few months we have had an extra six million dollars that I don't know where it came from. So, I had Jasmine, Cordial, B-More, and Shady to do a count on their units and income. I also went over the books from PA all the way down to DC. I'm trying to see where this *genie in a bottle* came from that dropped this six million on us."

100

Kareem took a sip of his drink as he watched Malachi.

"You said six million?"P

"Yeah, in the last three months."

"What's the count on the kilos upstate New York?"

"Honestly, I don't know. I do know that they are pulling in 300 kilos a week and we are shipping out 150 to 200 a week. I don't know what's in stock up there."

Malachi pulled on his cigar as he considered the situation.

"I think it's about time we take a trip up there then. Don't you think?"

"Or we can call, Nicki? She's up there."

"She's not. She won't be back until next week. Plus, I would like to take a look at things myself. It's been a while since I been up there."

"When you trying to go up there?"

"What better time than now?"

Kareem took the last shot of his drink and placed his glass down on the table.

"Let's take a ride then."

Malachi stood and pulled on his cigar again. "Let's go."

***

Stacy stepped out of her Maybach and walked into the auto part garage in Harlem on 128th with both her bodyguards behind her. When she got to the back there were six men waiting on her and two guys on their knees with paper bags over their heads. She walked up to Wild-B and Dollar.

"What's going on that you need me down here and why are these two on their knees with their hands tied behind their backs with bags over their heads?

Wild-B pointed at both of them then took the bags off their heads.

"About a week ago, these two were back-biting, talking about they ain't eating. Then I saw this goofy ass nigga right here talking to them foul ass niggas in Rukus Park and this bitch ass nigga right here was talking sideways out his mouth about licking us."

Stacy looked at both of them.

"I know them Rukus Park niggas don't mind kicking a door in if the shit is set up, right?"

"You know I should have your mother, father, brother, sister and every fucking body you care about killed."

Stacy looked around the dim interior of the garage and took her sunglasses off.

"Y'all niggas are going to die a painful and very slow death. I don't know who you think you are fucking with, but I'm the right bitch. Pick them up and put them in chains over there. I want to see how much pressure it takes to pull the human body apart."

Both men started yelling as they were being dragged to the chains, kicking their feet. One of Stacy's guards kicked one of the guys in the face, knocking him out cold as they chained his hands and feet to the machine before pressing the button. The machine started pulling the chains taut, pulling his body. All you heard were cries and flesh being torn apart as blood from his body was spilling out on the floor. When his body was in two pieces, the machine stopped pulling. Stacy looked at the other one on the floor tied up.

"Hook his ass up too. He's going for the same fucking ride."

"Nicki, no, please... no!"

Stacy just looked at him.

"Nigga, I don't hear your fucking cries. You thought you were just a Billy Badass talking about kicking my door in. Fuck what you are talking about!"

Stacy watched as his body was pulled apart too. She looked at the facial expression on everyone that was standing around looking at them.

"Wild-B, you said he was talking to them Rukus Park niggas? I think they need to find out who the fuck I am. Drop their bodies off in the park and the next time you see them niggas posted up in Rukus Park getting money, rock-a-bye their asses. We are *gorillas* on the block. Let it be known!"

Stacy put her glasses back on and turned around and walked out of the garage with her head held high. Once back in the car, one of Stacy bodyguards looked at her.

"Nicki, you know this is going to bring heat to Harlem, right?"

"Good, let's set this bitch on fire. It's time they know who I am. This is me keeping my foot on their neck."

Chapter 23

Malachi walked into the warehouse on the farm with Kareem. Kareem looked around and waved Kimberly over to him and Malachi.

"Kimberly, I see things have changed here."

"Yes, a lot has over the last few months."

"Tell me what the girls are pulling in every week. How many kilos are they making?"

"We were pulling in 300 a week. Now we are pulling close to 400 a week."

Malachi and Kareem looked at each other.

"Kimberly, show us around."

"Yes sir."

Malachi and Kareem followed behind Kimberly.

"The cages over here are new. Nicki had all four of them put in a little over four months ago. The first cage is our stock of all the kilos we have right now."

Malachi walked to the cage and looked at the kilos then at Kimberly.

"Two questions: Why is there no stamp on these kilos and how many do we have in stock?"

Kareem walked to the cage and looked also.

"We have 2,500 in stock right now, sir. Nicki didn't want a stamp on them until they are ready to be shipped out."

Kimberly pulled the chain of the chart off the cage and showed Malachi. Malachi nodded as he looked over the papers on the clipboard.

"In this cage are the orders that are on standby waiting for payments to be completed. On this chart, it says where the orders are going and how many units. The green check means the payment is completed. The red x means still pending. When an order is paid for, we move them in this cage and put

104

the stamp on them, and vac bag every unit in sets of ten. Once that's done, we move them to the shipment cage and that's this one right here."

Malachi and Kareem couldn't say anything disparaging on how Nicki was running things.

"Kimberly, what are the two extra tables for over there?"

"We have eight more girls working for us now. That's how we were able to go from 300 to 400 kilos in a week, sir."

"Kimberly, how many units are being shipped out a month?"

"Between New York City, Long Island, New Jersey, PA, and all the way down to DC, 3,200. Malachi, that's why we needed the extra girls to keep orders going out on time."

"And where did the extra girls come from? Did Nicki pull them out of the Diamond Playhouse?"

"No, a few of the girls here told Nicki that they had friends and family members that would work, and she reached out to Mrs. Blanka. Mrs. Blanka made it possible for them to get here."

"How long have they been here for?"

"Four months now, sir."

"Thank you, Kimberly. That will be all."

Malachi walked to his office on the farm. Once inside Malachi lit a cigar.

"Malachi, did you sign off for Nicki to have more girls brought up here or to reach out to Mrs. Blanka or any of the other things she's doing up here?"

"Kareem, Nicki has things in order. She's keeping orders coming and she changed the whole layout of the warehouse. She has things organized to keep count of everything plus the six million dollars that you don't know where it came from. So, that *genie in the bottle* might be Nicki."

"I just don't want her to overstep her boundaries and reaching out to Mrs. Blanka is one of them."

"I told her to keep operations tight up here and she is doing that better than before. I will talk to her about what boundaries not to cross."

"And the six million dollars?"

"I'll check her about that too."

Kareem nodded, knowing not to question Malachi, but he didn't like the freedom that Nicki was having. She was moving and changing things around and making calls without checking with him first. That was a spit in the face like she didn't have to answer to him no more now that Malachi was back.

***

Agent Dawn walked into Rukus Park up to the crime scene where Nicki's guys dumped both ripped apart bodies in the middle of the park on the court. He looked around at all the people and the police walking around. That's when he spotted Captain Fuller walking his way.

"You are a little far from home, Captain."

"You bet your ass, I am. This is Stacy Hall's stomping grounds. She is riding around in a Maybach along with two bodyguards like you said. They gorilla bred her, and I think she is claiming Harlem as her turf now. These two bodies right here had been ripped apart, I think it's the start of what is gonna prove to be a bloody summer."

"You might be fucking right."

"I overheard one of the detectives telling one of the officers nobody seen nothing. Remind you of something, Dawn?"

"Yeah, it reminds me of a few incidences with no witnesses."

"Sounds like the work of Malachi Williams, and the Black Diamond Cartel, Mr. Untouchable, the man who beat us in court. This motherfucker brought a man's child to court and threatened her life in front of all of us. We didn't know he had two detectives kidnapped in New York City in broad daylight and detectives killed in apartment buildings. Now we have two dead bodies ripped apart in Ruckus Park. This motherfucker keeps getting through the cracks."

"Captain, his day is coming, whether that means prison or a body bag I'm not sure, but his day is coming."

Captain Fuller looked at the dead bodies one more time before walking off.

"Where you going now, Fuller?"

"To get a drink."

"It's 10:00 am."

"I just saw two dead bodies ripped apart and their guts on the ground. My morning is already fucked up."

Agent Dawn looked at the bodies one more time before walking off.

"Wait up. I'm coming with you, what the hell?"

Chapter 24

Stacy was sitting at her kitchen table eating a fruit plate when her phone went off. She looked and seen it was Malachi calling her.

"Hey, what's up? Is everything alright?"

"Yeah, it is. What would make you ask that?" Malachi said, stepping out the back seat of the limo as he walked into Whitney Plaza up to the elevator.

"Because it's ten in the morning and you never called me this early before."

Malachi let out a light laugh.

"I'm calling because we need to talk."

"Over the phone or you want me to come to the farm?"

"I want you to open the front door to your penthouse. I'm at the door."

Malachi hung up after he said that. Stacy couldn't believe what he just said. She never told him about the penthouse or anybody else for that matter. She walked to the front door and opened it to see Malachi standing there in his $3,000 dollar Armani suit lighting a cigar.

"Please come in."

Malachi stepped through the doorway and looked around as Stacy closed the door behind him. Stacy's penthouse was laced out. All of her furniture was designer. Her living room was all white even her $2,500 cashmere area rug. She had a 72 inch flat screen tv on the wall above her fireplace. On the other wall, she had a big picture of the globe with big words around it. It said, "the world is yours," just like the one on Scarface. Malachi was beyond impressed.

"Malachi, how did you know I was here?"

"Nicki, I own New York. I know everything."

Stacy just nodded, knowing one of her guards had told him.

"Come have a seat at the dining room table."

Malachi sat at the table as Stacy went and got him an ashtray. She handed him the ashtray and sat across from him.

"So, what is it you want to talk about?"

"I was at the farm this week and I respect what you did up there."

"Thank you."

"But you never got the green light to have more females come up here from Mexico or to reach out to Mrs. Blanka. That was overstepping your boundaries."

"If I overstepped my boundaries, I apologize for that, but I have been keeping the numbers to everything. If I didn't have the girls sent up here we would have been working the girls that we currently have twice as hard. You told me to continue operations in upstate New York and I did. I didn't know you wanted me to call you every time the wind blows in a different direction."

"You are making a good point, but me and Kareem weren't kept in the loop on anything. We were left completely in the dark."

"Kareem was in the dark because he wasn't paying attention. You were in the dark because Kareem was slacking on his job. We are having this conversation because I was doing my job 100 percent. Just like how I been paying my 25%, there should be 6 million dollars in the account you gave me."

Malachi pulled his cigar and nodded.

"There was."

Stacy got up and walked to the living room. Malachi followed behind her as he looked out the window at the city of New York.

"Malachi, you said you own New York City, but the whole east coast you own the deadliest cartel. Let's be honest with each other. A nine year old child could pick up a gun and kill when somebody's in his ear telling him what to do, but on his own, he would be lost."

"What's the point you are trying to make, Nicki?"

"Kareem, Jasmine, Shady, B-More, and Cordial are all loyal and devoted to *you*, not the Black Diamond Cartel. Without your voice in their ears, they would be lost. Cordial and Shady would've never went to New Jersey. Kareem would've never had me killed those four females. Jasmine would've never helped you in Texas. The point that I'm making is you gave me a pass and when you opened your eyes, your money was there like you asked me. You and the Black Diamond Cartel aren't even a topic of conversation with the people I deal with. The puppet only exists because of the puppet master, without the puppet master, the puppet would just be a dead doll without you pulling the strings."

"Where everyone else exists is my point?"

Malachi knew Nicki was speaking facts. No one did what she did without him coaching them along. Nicki knew she had Malachi by the way he was looking out the window at the city. Nicki placed her hand on Malachi's cheek and turned his face to hers as she looked into his eyes.

"You don't ever have to question my loyalty to you or my devotion to the cartel. All I want is to see you win. Remember, I am your stamp." Nicki kissed Malachi's lips as she had her hand on his face. She stepped back and looked at him.

"You once kissed me and said it was a seal of trust between us. I just kissed you back and that's a kiss of loyalty as our foundation between us. I promise, I got you."

Malachi didn't say anything. He just kissed Nicki's forehead and walked out of her penthouse. Nicki walked to her dining room table and picked up her phone. After a few seconds her driver picked up.

"Hey, Cali, I was thinking, how about you and G have lunch with me around 1pm?"

"Sure thing, Nicki. I will let G know."

"Good." Nicki hung up. She knew what she had to do at 1pm because you couldn't serve two masters. You would be loyal to one and disloyal to the other one and G was disloyal to her for Malachi, and that was a deadly mistake.

***

"Shady, we are going all the way off the chart with this one tonight. I have it set up where both Detectives Mark and Clark are going to meet us in the warehouse parking lot next to the dumps. Be ready, because tonight, we are laying their asses down if they are not getting with our program."

Shady nodded as he smoked his blunt and sat in the Benz talking to Cordial.

"So we just going to leave the bodies there after we clap them?"

Shady passed the blunt to Cordial.

"Yeah, we are going to set their car on fire and get the fuck out of there. We are going to let them Patterson Ave niggas take the fall."

"What about Malachi?"

"He gave us New Jersey, so we move how we want to move."

"Sayless then. It's get down or lay down. You know I'm always with the bullshit."

"I already know."

Cordial started the Benz up and glanced at the watch on his wrist.

"Yoo, it's 12:30. I need to make a drop off. You trying to ride?"

"Shit, pull off. We out."

"Fucking right."

***

Stacy walked out of the plaza with G behind her. Once outside Cali was standing at the car with the back door open for her to get in. She stopped and looked at Cali.

"Cali, we are going to eat at Nicki's diner today."

"Yes ma."

Stacy got into the Maybach as G and Cali got in the front seats. Stacy pulled her phone out and called Drumma. After a few rings he picked up.

"Nicki, what's the word?"

"Did y'all take care of the Rukus Park yet?"

"Wild-B and Dollar going to make that box office hit, but them bum ass niggas haven't been up there since them pull apart toys been dropped off there."

"Drumma, find out where they are. No safe house in Harlem and when you find them, make that movie."

"Already on it now."

"Good, I hope to hear something in two days."

Stacy hung up the phone as her car was pulling in the back of Nicki's diner. Cali stopped the car and G opened the back door for her to get out. They all walked to a private table in the back room where their food was already waiting for them.

"Thank you for this lunch, Nicki."

Stacy smiled.

"Cali, you been with me for the last six months and G, you been by my side for the last few weeks. Both of you are loyal and I respect that. You know I never knew this was going to be the life for me two and a half years ago. I was kidnapped as soon as I walked out the subway. I was dragged to a hoe house. I was fucked and raped by all kinds of men. I seen females killed and beheaded in front of me. In that hoe house, every day was something new. A new scream, a new cry, I was taken from that house and put on a farm to watch more innocent females pick and make kilos of cocaine. When they fucked up, they were beat and banished to that hoe house or the Diamond Playhouse as they call it. I was forced to kill four females whose only crimes were their loved ones were looking for them. My family has been threatened to be killed if I didn't knuckle down and play ball. Then Malachi looked me in the eye and told me I have been gorilla bred. I was branded like a fucking animal. I was broken down to the lowest part of my life. Everyday, I looked in the mirror at my reflection till it hit me that *Stacy* is dead. I was reborn *Nicki*. The Black Diamond Cartel is my family now, so I'm the baddest and the deadliest bitch now."

Cali and G looked at Stacy as she talked, eating and drinking their Moet without saying a word.

"I call all my soldiers in Harlem my gorillaz, my apes. I was gorilla bred so it's my right to have gorillaz and apes under me. Two things I learned from The Black Diamond Cartel."

Stacy got up and walked around the table to Cali and put her arms over his shoulders, touching his chest with her hands.

"The first thing I learned is you can't stop the rain when it starts to pour."

She kissed the side of Cali's face before moseying over to G and putting her hands over his shoulders, touching his chest as well.

"The second thing I learned is loyalty comes with a price."p

She kissed G's cheek then she pulled her knife out and cut his throat from ear to ear. Then she pushed his upper body on top of the table then walked back to her seat. Cali put his glass down and just looked at G.

"You know what, Cali? I forgot about the 3rd thing. You can't serve two masters because you will be loyal to one and disloyal to the other one. G chose loyalty to Malachi. He was spying on me, running back and telling Malachi everything I was doing. G's loyalty to Malachi was death by my hands."

"How do you know that?"

"Malachi came to my penthouse. Only two people know where I live, you and G. Did I kill the wrong person, Cali?"

"No, Nicki. I'm loyal to you."

"I know you are. Let's finish eating before our food gets cold."

Stacy looked at G's dead body on the table and his eyes were looking right at her as she sipped on her Moet, smiling at his dead body. Cali knew now that Stacy truly was a coldhearted killer.

***

Shady stood in front of the BMW smoking a blunt as the black Ford pulled up. He watched as Detective Mark and Detective Clark stepped out of the car and walked over to him. Both detectives looked at him.

"Where is Cordial at?"

Shady pulled his blunt. "He had some other shit to take care of that needed to be done yesterday."

Detective Clark nodded.

"Look, the long and short of it is we are paying y'all a lot of money. The free ride is over from here on out. Y'all work for *us*. This ain't no negotiation conversation. It's a deal or no deal."

Detective Mark looked around. Something just didn't feel right. He walked up to Shady.

"Deal. We ain't doing no dirty work, but we will give you a heads up on raids, investigations, and we will be your eyes on the inside."

"Nigga, that works for me."

Shady reached into his pocket and pulled out two envelopes and handed them to Detective Mark.

"There's $50,000 in both of them. Next payment in 5 months."

Shady turned around and walked to his car, got in, and pulled off. Mark handed the envelope to Detective Clark.

"What the fuck you make that deal for, Mark?"

"Look around, Clark. This wasn't no fucking meeting. This was where the Patterson boys be. They kill us, the Patterson boys take the fall, and them Diane Project niggas are good. Fucking right I took the deal. $120,000 a year just for some info or a heads up. Clark, it's a win -win for both of us and the best part, right now, we are walking out of here $50,000 richer."

"You know the door you just opened?"

"Yeah, one that makes sure we live another day and that we ain't in a black bag tonight. Come on... let's get the fuck out of here."

Once they got in the car and pulled off, Cordial stepped out from the other side of the dumpster with his AR-15 in his hands and gunfire shattered the tranquility.

Chapter 25

Malachi looked out the window at the farm as he smoked his cigar. He was waiting on everyone to arrive for the meeting. Turning around when he heard the door open, he saw Kareem walking through the door, strolling up to him, and giving him a pound and hug.

"I'ma take the lead in this meeting today, Kareem. Who all are here right now?"

"I saw everyone's car outside. I believe they are in the greenhouse office waiting on you."

"Come on… let's not keep them waiting then."

Malachi and Kareem walked to the greenhouse office. When they walked through the doors Shady and Cordial were playing pool. Jasmine was talking with B-More. When everyone saw Malachi, they stopped what they were doing and sat at the table. Malachi looked around then at Kareem.

"Where's Nicki?"

"I didn't know you wanted her here."

"Why wouldn't I have her here? She is a part of this cartel."

Malachi pulled his phone out and called Stacy. After a few seconds she picked up.

"Where are you at?"

"In my office going over the shipments for this month."

"Drop what you are doing and come to the greenhouse office. We are having a meeting right now."

"I'm on my way."

Malachi looked at Kareem.

"Kareem, when I call a meeting, I want everyone here."

Nobody had seen Stacy in over a year, but Malachi. When the doors opened Malachi's two blue pit-bulls ran into the office up to him. Stacy sashayed into the office looking like Ashanti with her honey blonde hair as it came down her face in curls all over her caramel skin tone. She had on a white Prada dress that hugged her hourglass body with a diamond cut out of the right side of her dress, showing her diamond stamp with the letters *BDC* in cursive. She had a tattoo around the stamp that said, *loyalty, devotion, dedicated.* She had on open-toe two inch Prada shoes. The diamonds she was wearing looked like water around her neck and water drops on her ears. Once she sat at the table, one of Malachi's dogs ran up to her and she patted him on the head while looking at everyone.

"I apologize to everyone for my late arrival. I didn't know we had a meeting here today."

Malachi looked at her.

"It's ok. You weren't informed."

Cordial tapped Shady on the leg as he eyed Stacy, with Shady giving him a look like *damn.*

"Now that everybody is here, let's get started. Cordial, how are operations in New Jersey?"

Malachi pulled on his cigar as he looked at him.

"Good... we are pulling in three million every drop. Now that we have the boys from Patterson Ave shopping with us, we are about to put the whole city on lock."

Malachi nodded.

"Jasmine, how are your operations going?"

"From the apartments to the three sports bars and hotel, we are pulling in 2.5 a month."

Malachi looked at B-More and nodded.

"With the Diamond Playhouse, the girls are pulling in $500,000 a month."

"Nicki, how are things here?"

"With the new girls I had brought up here, we are pulling 400 kilos a week. Operations are shipping out 2,500 kilos a month from New York to PA to DC, and pretty soon Florida. The numbers are growing. Soon we may have to have more girls brought up to keep orders filled."

"We not only took over the city, but we are taking over the entire east coast. Everyone will keep their operations as usual. I have some obligations that need my immediate attention. Kareem is my number 2. Everyone at this table knows that already. I'm headed down to Mexico to see Mrs. Blanka. Kareem, Nicki, let me have a word with you two in private."

Malachi got up from the table and walked to the far side of the room with Nicki and Kareem. Jasmine observed them as they were talking.

"Kareem, Nicki has the farm. She already knows before she reaches out to any other cartel to talk with you first. She's only obligated to be at the farm four days out of the week. Nicki, Kareem is my number two. He's my face when I'm not here. I don't know how long I will be gone. Kareem, you have the crown to this empire. Kareem, just so we are clear, Nicki has the farm. Nicki, Kareem is my face. He's wearing the crown. Now Nicki, let me talk with Kareem one on one."

"Sure thing." Nicki walked off to the window, knowing Malachi just let Kareem know the farm was hers.

"She by herself. Shady, pull up on her."

"Yeah, I think I'm about to make that happen right now." Shady walked over to Nicki at the window.

"I see you, Nicki, hands down."

Before Nicki could say anything, both of Malachi's blue pit-bulls trotted over to her and sat down on each side of her, looking at Shady, growling low under their breaths. Nicki bent down and looked at them as she placed her hand on their heads.

"It's ok, boys. Go play."

Once she said that, both dogs trotted off.

"I'm sorry about that. They are a little overprotective of me."

"I see that."

118

Kareem eyeballed Malachi when they saw that.

"The farm ain't all she has now."

Malachi ain't say nothing as he lit his cigar and walked out the office. Both of his dogs ran out behind him. Kareem just looked at Nicki and cut his eyes at her, letting her know he did not like her.

Chapter 26

Drama sat across the street on the steps as Wild-B and Dollar paced the block on the other side of the street. Mayham was parked down the block in a Ford Explorer watching the Rukus Park niggas all posted up on the steps smoking weed, drinking 40's, and talking shit to each other. Wild-B looked at Drama and nodded. Drama put his hoodie on and pulled his gun out on the low. Dollar and Wild-B were walking past them nonchalantly.

Dollar yelled out, "Nicki said what's up."

All you heard were the gunshots erupt as Dollar and Wild-B let off the Mac-11 and 9mm, shooting everyone on the steps. One of the guys ran in the streets. Drama ran up on him as he was looking back at Wild-B and Dollar and put his 45 to his stomach and said, "Bang bang, motherfucker. We are the gorillaz and apes on the block," as he let the 45 bullets rip through ol' boy's stomach, causing him to fall on the ground, and Drama shot him three more times in the head. Mayham pulled up on them and yelled, "Come on! We have to get the fuck up out of here now!"

Everyone got in the truck as Mayham pulled off, leaving all six of them dead. Nicki was showing Harlem she wasn't to be fucked with and her gorillaz and apes were pulling up. Talking *wasn't* an option.

***

Malachi stepped off the plane and got into the car Mrs. Blanka had waiting on him. He sat quietly in the backseat, smoking his cigar as he rode to Mrs. Blanka's house. When the car pulled up, Mrs. Blanka was outside waiting on him. Once he stepped out of the car, she smiled and walked up to him and gave him a hug and kiss on the cheek as she wrapped her arm around his and started walking.

"Malachi, come walk with an old lady in the garden. We have much to talk about."

"Indeed, we do, Mrs. Blanka."

"Tell me, how your trip was down here?"

***

Nicki sat in her living room watching the news about the six men killed in Harlem as she sipped on her Moet. She had no doubt that Drama wouldn't get the job done. Harlem was her city now and her press game was real. She knew Malachi was gone for the next few months because she got into his ear. She also knew Kareem was going to be a problem, but she was ready for whatever. She had purchased an auto part garage, a diner, and a used car lot over the last few months. She had been storing kilos like a squirrel preparing for winter, with 2,500 stashed away that nobody knew about. The females she asked Mrs. Blanka to help her bring upstate were for her. All the orders were on time. She just made it look good in Malachi's eyes. He made *her*. He *gorilla bred* her and there was no turning back. She was the bitch that wore Prada. The deadliest and baddest and she had something to prove. Not only did Mrs. Blanka help her get the girls, but she also schooled her on a few things as well.

***

"When Nicki asked me to help bring the girls to New York, I told her that the trafficking fee for humans is $4,000 a head. She was very respectful and had no problem with that. She did a wire transfer within an hour. Why do you ask me about her? That was so many months ago."

"I was just making sure she was respectful to you. That's all. It slipped my mind with everything I had going on in New York."

"Malachi, I have been in this business for a very long time, and I know bullshit when I hear it. What is the real reason you asked me that question?"

Malachi took a deep breath. "She was talking about the cartel on *Wake Up New York*, so I had her kidnapped. I put her in the hoe house where she was raped. I made her oversee the cocaine operations. I had her kill four innocent people. I threatened her family's lives. I gorilla bred her in the worst way, and within the last two years, she has done more for my cartel than anybody else. She has been loyal, devoted, and dedicated."

Mrs. Blanka sipped the tea she had on the table as they sat in the garden talking.

"Malachi, she is going to be more ruthless and devoted to you because of what you put her through. She is an *apex predator* now. How she thinks and moves is because of the pain and hurt *you* put her through."

"So, how do I control an apex predator?"

"You don't let them kill and eat off the land. You are *the head* of your own cartel. You don't need to be seen or heard from, from anybody. You show your face to your round table and make the calls without you being there. That's what a boss does."

Malachi nodded.

"Plus, I could use you down here with me for a while. I have a feeling your cartel is going to be just fine functioning without you for a while."

Malachi didn't say anything by way of a response. He lowered his head and lit his cigar.

"Another thing, a shark is an apex predator and you can't control a shark."

Chapter 27

"Captain Fuller, did you see the mess in Harlem last night?"

Captain Fuller took a sip of his coffee and shook his head at Agent Dawn.

"What happened out there?"

Agent Dawn placed a file with some pictures on his desk. Captain Fuller picked the file up and started going through it.

"A local crew was killed."

Captain Fuller was looking at the pictures.

"Agent Dawn, this was a set up. They didn't know this was going to happen."

"Yeah, exactly my point. Not only that, look at the last picture I have there."

Captain Fuller picked up the picture of Gray Baker dead with his throat cut open from ear to ear.

"Does he look familiar to you, Fuller?"

"Yeah, but I can't put my finger on it, Dawn."

Agent Dawn reached into his top pocket and pulled out three more pictures and passed them to Captain Fuller.

"You have to be fucking kidding me. He was one of Stacy's bodyguards? I remember this picture from the investigation room."

"It's funny everyone who is circling around Stacy Hall is dead, bodies ripped apart and dropped off in Rukus Park. The Rukus Park crew dead and now one of her bodyguards."

Before Captain Fuller could reply there was a knock at his office door and a female officer was standing there.

"Sir?"

"Yes, officer?"

"Stacy Hall was just seen going into the sub restaurant off of 114th street in Brooklyn."

Agent Dawn and Captain Fuller both got up.

"Thank you, officer. Dawn, I think it's time we both go have a word with Stacy. What you say?"

"I say you read my mind."

Both men marched out of the office. Within 20 minutes, they both was at the entrance of the sub restaurant.

"Nicki, two detectives just walked in here."

Nicki checked and saw who it was and then waved the waiter over to her.

"Yes, Ms. Nicki?"

"Bring me two more glasses and a bottle of Moet on ice."

"Yes ma'am."

Captain Fuller saw her at the back of the restaurant.

"She's over there, Dawn… at the back table."

Agent Dawn and Captain Fuller started walking her way, right up to her table. Nicki placed her fork down and peered at them.

"Stacy Hall or Nicki Guns, which one would you prefer?"

"Captain Fuller, food is very important to me, and you stopped me from eating. What can I do for you?"

At that time the waiter walked back to the table with two glasses and a bottle of Moet.

"Can you please pour Captain Fuller and Agent Dawn a glass please?"

"Yes, ma'am."

Captain Fuller and Agent Dawn pulled out a chair and sat at the table with Nicki.

"Stacy or Nicki, we know you are making a name for yourself in Harlem. People are getting killed."

Nicki ain't say nothing, just picked up her glass of Moet and took a sip.

"Stacy, we don't know what happened to you when you were kidnapped, but this is not you."

"Captain, people die and get killed all the time. How that song goes: *you can't stop the rain when it starts to pour.*"

"So, I guess it was raining in Harlem when the eight guys were killed out there, two dumped in Rukus Park. Two weeks later, six more killed that used to be in Rukus Park."

"I saw and read about that in the newspaper."

"Did you read about Gary Baker in the newspaper as well?"

Nicki let out a little laugh. Agent Dawn looked at Cali then back at Nicki.

"No, what happened to Gary? Is he alright?"

"If you call getting your throat cut open and dumped on the side of the road, then yeah."

"That's sad, but it teaches us to watch the company we keep, Captain Fuller."

"What about the four innocent females hung alive outside of my office window?"

"It could have been someone's mother, beautiful wife of fifteen years, handsome son and their pretty daughter. Some people don't get the picture until it starts to rain. Then it's too late, period."

"Did you just threaten my family?"

Nicki just looked as Agent Dawn put his hand on Fuller's shoulder.

"Fuller, I think it's time for us to go."

Captain Fuller stood up and bent over looking at Nicki. "History lesson, John Gotti, Sammy the Bull, Al Capone were all talking just like you. Now they are *dead.*"

"Captain Fuller, you just told me about a rat— John Gotti, an informer— Sammy the Bull, and a traitor Al Capone. I could've flipped a two headed penny and bet on tails that they all were going to die. It's a good thing I'm not a part of them noodle eating mafia motherfuckers."

"I'll see you soon, Nicki Guns."

Nicki eyed them as they walked away.

"Nicki, that cop is going to be a problem."

"I already know, but we don't want to start killing cops right now."

***

"So, you're telling me this Ashanti looking bitch the same one who was talking about us on *Wake Up New York*, sucking dick and fucking in the hoe house is walking around like a boss up bitch now and Malachi is rocking with this?"

Kareem walked up to Jasmine and passed her a glass of gin and juice as they talked in the private room at the club Jasmine owned.

"I don't know what the fuck her and Malachi have going on, but he is loyal as fuck to this bitch right now. I could see it in his eyes when he looked at her at the meeting the other day."

"So, you think he's fucking her?"

"No, he ain't fucking her, but I can't put my finger on what the fuck they have going on. He did put her in her place in front of me. I will say that."

"So, won't you pull up on her and try to figure her out"

"She is not going to open that door, but I'm done talking about her. How you looking down here?"

Kareem drifted to the double-sided window in Jasmine's office in the private room in the back of the club and looked out of it, overseeing the club. Jasmine walked up next to him.

"Malachi is gone be out the picture for the next few months. This is your show now. Let it be known. He gave you the keys to the cartel."

Kareem took his glass and tapped Jasmine's and drank to what she just said before turning his attention back to the club's floor.

126

Chapter 28

"The girls are $1,500 for two hours. There's no negotiation. That's the entrance fee and the girl you choose."

"What about race?"

"This is the candy shop. We have all races. Whatever you like. We have it. If she's not here, we can get her here for the right price."

The fat white dude nodded. "So how much will it cost me to window shop to see if the girl I want is here?"

"It's $750.00 just to walk in these doors and the other $750.00 is for your two hours of pleasure. You ready for your tour of The Diamond Playhouse or as I like to call it, the Candy Shop?"

"Yeah, I'm ready."

The man handed B-More $750.00 before traveling into the building. He looked at all the girls behind the door through the glass window.

"Hey, if I don't see the one I like, how much will it cost me to get the one I want?"

"$5,000... it costs money to play."

"Ok, because I don't see none I like. I'll call you in a few days and tell you who I like."

"I'll be waiting on your call."

B-More walked him to the doors then went back inside. Dereck walked up to him.

"Yoo, where you know him from?"

"One of the regulars, Randy, brought him to me last week and said he spent good money."

"Cool. I know Randy been coming here for a while."

The fat white man got into the tv satellite van down the street.

"How it looks in there Detective Gorden?"

"Like a rapist's playhouse. There's about 15 females in there and they don't have no problem kidnapping the girl you want for the right price. He made that clear."

"Yeah, we know. We have it all on tape."

"So, what you want to do now?"

"We set a sting for the kidnapping then at the same time, we kick the door in."

"Let's get the ball rolling then."

***

Nicki sat at the back table in her diner eating and drinking a cup of coffee as she read the newspaper. When a light skinned man with a red shirt and blue jeans walked in the diner,

he scanned around then walked to her table. Cali stood up and stopped him as he tried to get to Nicki.

"Hey, do you know her?"

Nicki placed the cup of coffee and the newspaper down and viewed the man.

"No, but I got some information that might open the door for me to get to know her."

"Cali, let him have a seat. I could always use information."

Cali patted him down to make sure he didn't have a gun on him then pulled the chair out so he could sit across from Nicki.

"Two things, eating is very important to me, so I don't like my time being wasted, and two, I only want to hear facts."

"I respect that, and I will only speak facts We are in Manhattan and my connections go all the way to the Bronx. There's a big sting that's going down next week at the Diamond Playhouse. They know there's 15 plus females in there and that it costs $5,000 to kidnap the girl you want. It

128

also costs $1,500 dollars for two hours with the girl of your choice."

Nicki looked at Cali then back at the man sitting in front of her.

"What did you say your name was again?"

"My name is Roger, but my friends call me Mac."

"How do you know all of this?"

"Because I'm an officer with the 27th Precinct and Brooklyn is my department's investigation."

"How do you know to come tell me this?"

"Because your picture is on the bulletin board. They think you are a part of the Diamond Cartel, but there's no fact to that right now. They know you are operating in Harlem and more about the Diamond Playhouse. B-More's real name is Mike Powell. They have him on tape talking about the price of kidnapping. They are planning a sting to kidnap a young girl undercover."

"Why are you bringing this to me?"

"To show you how valuable I can be… for the right price."

Nicki nodded. "Do you have a number?"

"Yeah." Roger passed her the card with his number on it.

"Mac, I will be in touch."

"I'll be waiting to hear from you."

Nicki picked up the card and tapped it twice on the table as Max walked out the diner. She picked up her cell phone and called Kareem. After a few seconds Kareem picked up the phone.

"Yeah, what's up?"

"I think I need to check on B-More in the Diamond Playhouse. Word is he brought an undercover in there."

"Look, B-More know what he doing. He's been running that spot way before you were in there. You just worry about the farm." Kareem hung up after saying that and quickly called B-More and B-More picked up right away.

"What's the word, Kareem?"

"Shit, I'm just checking on you seeing how things are going down there. That's all."

"Man, this shit is smooth like a baby's ass. I'm a hundred down here."

"Cool, stay on point."

"Copy that."

Kareem hung up the phone and lit his cigar. Nicki might have Malachi under her spell, but she ain't talking about shit with him. He didn't trust or give two shits about her.

Chapter 29

Nicki sat down at her dining room table as she played with the card Roger gave her a few days ago, thinking about if she should call him or not. She picked up her phone and dialed his number as she walked to her penthouse living room window, looking outside as it rained. Roger picked up after a few rings.

"Hello?"

"Let's say the information you gave me is true. How long before this sting goes down?"

"Tomorrow before 1pm. If you are going to make a move, it needs to be tonight."

"How can I get in without being seen?"

"All I can tell you is you have to go in through the back somehow because they are watching all the movement in the front."

"What about the sting on B-More, setting him up with the undercover officer?"

"They aren't worried about that no more. They already got him on tape, but they still might try something. I don't know."

"I'll be in touch, Mac."

Nicki hung up the phone and called her driver. After a few seconds he picked up the phone.

"Yes ma'am?"

"Come get me and bring the van. Make sure you have your gun."

"Yes ma'am. I'm on the way."

***

"Wait here in the van and be ready to drive when I come back. Do not leave the van."

"I got you, Nicki."

Nicki got out of the van and walked through the cut. She stepped through a hole in the gate at the back of the Diamond Playhouse that led up to the back door. She knocked two times on the back door before Dereck opened it and gawked at her.

"What are you doing here?"

"I will explain that later, but right now, we have to get the girls out of here. They are about to raid tomorrow."

"How do you know this?"

"Because a few days ago, B-More brought an undercover cop in here and he has him on tape talking about everything."

"I fucking knew that fat bastard was a pig from the moment I saw him."

"Dereck, we can talk about that later. We have to move *now*."

Dereck started opening the doors to the rooms as Nicki took the girls to the van two at a time.

"Cali, I have four more girls I have to get. I'll be right back."

"I'm waiting on you."

Nicki walked back through the cut to the Diamond Playhouse. Once inside she saw Dereck arguing with B-More at the front door of the Diamond Playhouse with *the same* fat white man as before. She overheard Dereck yell, "He's a cop," causing B-More to look at him. That's when the undercover officer pulled out his gun. Nicki saw him and pulled her gun and shot at him, hitting the cop in the chest and making him fall back out the door. B-More saw blue and red lights coming his way, so he withdrew his gun and started shooting at them. Nicki frowned as Dereck opened every door and shot every girl in the head twice, killing them. Nicki ran up to him.

"What are you doing?"

"They know too much, too many faces."

Nicki took off running back to the van. B-More closed the front door, locking it, and ran to the back room, retrieved the gallon of gas, and started pouring it all over the Diamond Playhouse. That's when the door was kicked in. Dereck went to shoot but was gunned down by the police. B-More dropped a match, setting the place on fire. He ducked down the side of the door and called Kareem, who picked up after a few rings.

"Kareem, the Diamond Playhouse been hit by the police."

All Kareem heard in the background was gunshots.

"B-More, what the fuck is going on?"

"Come get me. Meet me in the back two blocks over on Lincoln Ave."

"I'll be there in 20 minutes."

B-More put the phone in his pocket and tried to run out the back door when he was shot in the leg and shoulder, falling to the floor. He got back up, shooting at the officers. The Diamond Playhouse was full of black smoke. By the time he made it out the back door to the gate, he fell, sitting down on the ground and shooting at the police coming his way. Kareem stopped the car and jumped out on Lincoln Ave. He ran to the gate and saw all the officers coming his way to get B-More. B-More lifted his gun to shoot but was out of bullets. Nicki ran to the side of Kareem, prompting him to look at her.

"Kareem, there is no way he can get out of this. You know what you have to do."

"I'm *not* killing him, Nicki. He's loyal. He's solid."

Nicki looked at Kareem before running up to the gate and yelling B-More's name.

"B-More!" When he turned around, she shot him three times in the chest, instantly killing him.

Kareem couldn't believe what she just did. She shot twice at the police and took off running back to the van. Kareem ran to his car and pulled off. Both of them got out of there. The Diamond Playhouse was up in flames. Dereck was killed as well as the four girls. Nicki killed B-More and shot a cop. She had called Kareem and told him about what went down but he didn't pay her no mind. Now they all had to face Malachi. The only good thing was that she had gotten ten girls out of there alive and she made the hard choice that Kareem couldn't.

Chapter 30

"What the fuck you telling me? *Nicki* bodied B-More?"

"Jasmine, she looked dead at me and said, 'you know what you have to do.' I told her, 'I'm not killing him.' That's when she ran to the gate and called his name and popped him three times."

"She bumped her fucking head and lost her marbles. What the fuck was she thinking?"

"I don't know." Kareem looked at his phone when it was going off, noticing that it was Malachi calling him.

"This is Malachi. Hold on, Jasmine." He picked up the phone.

"I got the 225 page. What's up?"

"The Diamond Playhouse was hit. Dereck is dead. B-More is dead, and I don't know how many girls are alive."

"What the fuck you mean, the Diamond Playhouse was hit and B-More and Dereck are dead, and you don't know how many of my girls are alive?"

"Shit got ugly, Malachi."

"I want everybody on the farm by 3pm tomorrow afternoon." Malachi hung up the phone in a state of rage.

***

"How is Detective Gorden doing?"

"He's good, Captain. He should be home in the next few days."

"That's good news, so tell me, what we got?"

"We have two dead males, a Mike Powell, AKA, B-More shot 6 times. Then we have Dereck Write shot two times and four Jane Doe's. The place was burned to the ground. We have no file, records, nothing. Everything went up in flames."

"You have to be *fucking* kidding me! Six dead bodies, one friendly shot, a burned building, and no fucking arrest money. Man, hours, and time fucking wasted. Get me all the reports on my desk ASAP, detective."

"Yes, Captain."

Captain Fuller strode back to his car after looking at the crime scene one more time.

***

Shady was smoking a blunt when his phone went off with a text message: ***meeting tomorrow afternoon at 3pm at the farm. Be there per Malachi.*** Shady got up and walked to the room where Cordial was.

"Yoo, we have a meeting tomorrow at the farm at 3pm per Malachi. I don't know what went down but this sounds real bad."

"Yoo, I just got that same text from Jasmine and Kareem."

"Yeah. It sounds like something went *boom*!"

"Here we go with the goofy shit."

"Who the fuck you telling? I'm bout to go finish smoking this blunt and counting this money up."

"Copy that."

Chapter 31

Nobody said a word as they all sat at the table. The tension was thick in the air. Kareem and Jasmine were glaring in each other's eyes from across the table. It was 2:28pm. The office door opened and Malachi stomped into the office. His facial expression showed he was pissed off. Walking to the top of the table and taking a seat, he looked directly at Kareem. With anger in his voice, he stated, "I was only gone a few weeks. I left you a multi-million dollar empire. Then I get a call from you saying one of my operations burned down, B-More and Dereck are dead, and you don't know how many of my girls are dead or alive. Kareem, you need *to talk* and I mean talk fast."

All eyes were on Kareem as he started speaking.

"B-More called me and said the Diamond Playhouse was being raided. He needed me to pick him up. I heard gunshots in the background and yelling. By the time I got there, I saw B-More shooting it out with the police. There was no way out for him. He was out of bullets just sitting on the ground. Then Nicki showed up out of nowhere, killed B-More, and took off running. I got the fuck out of there and here we are today."

Malachi cut his eye at Nicki and lashed out, "Your tongue works, right? Because you *really* need to start using it."

Nicki took a deep breath before telling her version of events.

"There's more to the story. I called Kareem a week ago and told him word got back to me that B-More had brought an undercover cop into the Diamond Playhouse. In so many words, Kareem told me to *fuck off* and that B-More was running that spot way before I was getting fucked in there. He hung up on me after saying that, so I did what I had to do. After reconfirming that things were in play for today and knowing that I had to make a move last night, I got two vans and parked two blocks over on Lincoln Ave. I went through the back of the Diamond Playhouse and talked to Dereck, telling him about the undercover cop and how the girls needed to be moved. He said he knew that motherfucker was a pig when he saw him, so he got into action and started opening the room doors while I got the girls out of there. When I was going back to get the other girls, Dereck and B-More were arguing at the front door with the cop. Then Dereck told B-More that the man was a cop, triggering the cop to pull out his gun, so I shot him and he fell out the door. B-More noticed the blaring lights outside and began shooting at the police as they were trying to come in and Dereck started killing the other girls. He said that they knew too much and knew too many faces. At that time, I had gotten the ten girls away from him. Then I saw Kareem pulling up and jumping out of his car, so I ran up to him, saw B-More's position, and told Kareem that he knew what he had to do. There was no way out for B-More, but Kareem said that he couldn't kill him because he was a loyal soldier, so I said *fuck it* and I did it."

That's when Kareem jumped up and pointed his finger at Nicki.

"Who the fuck were you to make that call? He was with us from day one."

Nicki leapt up and Malachi watched on, not saying a word as they were face to face.

"*I* made the hard choice. *He* fucked up. *You* fucked up. That's why we're here today, right now because of you!"

"You should have been dead when you were on tv talking about the cartel."

"So drop one in the chamber and shoot that bitch. Judgement day, I don't have no remorse for what I did and if I had to do it again, I would do it the same fucking way!"

"You know what, Nicki? You are about yourself. You don't know what loyalty is."

When Kareem said that, Nicki looked at everyone at the table and in a relaxed voice, replied, "Loyalty is making the hard choice to see the bigger picture. Jahem was arrested and became a state witness. He told secrets that got the devil's attention when the DA said 50 to 100 years. Did we really want to take that chance again with B-More honestly? Dereck killed four females because he said they knew too much. That was a risk that he wasn't going to take. He could've made it out of there alive, but he didn't. Why? Because he *protected* the cartel. He *protected* Malachi by killing them females and it cost him his life behind loyalty. Slim was loyal from the start, and he fucked up over some pussy he put before the cartel and fifteen females died behind his actions. That started a chain reaction that caught New York's attention. That had the feds knocking at Malachi's door. The hard choice over years of loyalty is he had to die no matter how you want to look at it, Kareem. Bishop jumped in front of two bullets for Cordial. His loyalty came with a death price. You all could look at me as the bad guy, but we don't know what B-More would've said in that investigation room when they start throwing numbers at him. Kareem, you said I don't know what loyalty is. By me killing B-More, *I* protected the cartel. *I* protected Malachi. *I* put the cartel first. *I* put Malachi first. *I* was loyal to the cartel, to Malachi. Loyalty comes with a price and B-More's price was death. This is the life that we live and the hard choice we have to make to protect the cartel." Nicki sat down after spewing that.

"Kareem, I don't know what your issues are with Nicki, but she called and told you about the undercover cop. You disrespected her. Then hung up the phone on her. She got ten girls out of there alive and she made the hard choice you *wouldn't* by killing B-More, by putting the cartel first. Kareem, you are *incapable* of running the cartel. Nicki, where are the girls?"

"In the back houses on the farm."

Malachi nodded.

"Everybody leave me but Kareem."

Everyone wandered out of the office as Malachi glowered at Kareem.

"You started this with me, but you are fucking up. The next time you fuck up, Kareem, I mean this... I *will* kill you." Malachi patted Kareem on the shoulder and got up and walked out the room.

Chapter 32

Malachi sat in his office smoking a cigar with his two stress balls in his hand when Cordial walked into his office.

"Malachi, can I have a word with you?"

"Yeah. What's up?"

"Nicki said some real shit at the meeting the other day and Kareem did fuck up. I'm not taking nobody's side here. I just want you to keep in mind that Kareem had been here from the very start before there was a cartel."

"I did keep that in mind. That's why he's still alive, but this is bigger than me and you. We have cartel ties that means we can't make mistakes. How is Jersey treating you and Shady out there?"

"Jersey was the move. Jersey showing us love."

"Cordial, I'm shutting the farm down. I'm going to Mexico. It's too hot right now to have that type of operation running with the feds knocking at our door. The only person they want is me. So if I have to leave to protect y'all and the cartel, then that's what I'm going to do."

"Malachi, fuck that. They kill you. They kill me. We're going out together."

"You and Shady are going to stay in New Jersey. Kareem and Jasmine have Brooklyn. Nicki will stay in Manhattan and the Bronx is an open turf. I'll supply everyone with 1,000 kilos at $17,000 a pop. I'm still going to be making calls, but you won't see my face. Everybody is going to be their own man. There is no more second in command. Kareem is incapable of that position, but everybody is still a part of the Black Diamond Cartel. My word is the beginning and the end. That's all that matters."

Cordial nodded. Malachi didn't want to leave New York, but loyalty came with a price. Before he saw anybody else in a grave for protecting him, he would protect them first by leaving. That was putting and protecting the cartel first. That was his loyalty to them.

Chapter 33

It'd been three weeks since Malachi shut down the farm. Jasmine walked up to Kareem as he sat at the bar drinking shots of Ciroc.

"You know, Jasmine, I been here from the start and Malachi let that bitch get in his ear to leave us all. Where the fuck is his loyalty at?"

"You know I had my moments with Malachi, but *he* left *us*. We never leave him. He never gave us a chance to show him our loyalty if our backs were against the wall and we were locked up, so you know what I'm thinking, Kareem?"

"No, tell me."

Jasmine put her arms around Kareem's neck and shoulders and whispered in his ear.

"Fuck him. Let's do our own thing, me and you. We have 2,000 kilos between the two of us."

"What about loyalty?"

"We are being loyal to what we have going on."

"You sure this is the road you want to take?"

Jasmine didn't say nothing. She kissed Kareem on the lips before talking. "Does that answer your question?"

"Yeah, it does." Kareem got up and kissed Jasmine. He walked her from the bar in his office to the couch in his office, laying her down as he got on top of her, kissing her soundly.

***

Nicki sat on her couch as both of Malachi's pit-bulls laid on the floor in front of her. When Malachi left, she kept both of them. She picked up the phone and called Roger, who picked up after a few rings.

"Hello."

"You have my attention now. We need to talk. Are you free right now?"

"Yes."

"Good, meet me at my diner. I'll be there in 45 minutes."

"I'll see you then."

Nicki hung up her phone, got dressed, and walked out of the lobby to her car. Cali was waiting for her.

"We are going to the diner, Cali," she informed him as she got in the back of the Maybach. Cali closed the door after she got inside.

***

"Yo, Drama, how we are looking over there, baby?"

"We caked all the way up. With them Rukus Park niggas flatlined, nigga, it's just bread and butter this way."

"Sayless, I'm about to pull up on baby girl."

"Dollar, you talking about Beckey with the good hair from the east side of Harlem?"

"Already."

"Dollar, you need to have her pull up over here. You going over there ain't the move knowing how we rocked them, baby. We gave them some permanent *NyQuil*."

"Them niggas don't want no smoke. They know how the gorillaz and apes move."

"Be on point, bro."

"Copy that fam."

"Yo, be on point."

Dollar walked off, putting his thumb in the air.

***

"Your information was on point. Thank you for that."

"You're welcome."

Nicki looked at Cali and nodded. Cali handed Roger a white envelope.

144

"There's $5,000 dollars in there. You will get that every month. I want updates on everything and all current investigations."

"You have my word. I'll keep you posted."

"Good."

Roger got up and walked away from the table.

"Nicki, do you trust him?"

"I have no choice now, do I?"

"I guess you don't."

***

"Baby, you have that water for real. Your box is too tight."

"You like this, lil Daddy. How I move my hips on this thick stick of yours?"

"Hell yeah. I'm trying to put a baby in you before the night is up."

"Go ahead, Daddy, crack my egg. Cum deep in this pussy."

Dollar had his back against the headboard as Candy was riding him. She had one foot on the floor and her arms wrapped around him. She turned his head to the mirror on the closet door so he could look at himself as she bounced on him harder and harder.

"Baby, cum in this pussy."

"I'm about to. Damn!"

Candy rode Dollar until he came all in her pussy.

"Yo, on God, you have that fucking water."

"I do, baby."

"Fucking right."

Candy kissed Dollar's forehead and then got off of him.

"I'm going to get something to drink. Do you want something to drink too?"

"Yeah, I could use something to drink after that ride."

"Ok, I'll be right back, Daddy."

Candy walked out of the room door as Dollar closed his eyes, catching his breath. When the door opened back up, two guys breezed into the room with guns out.

"Yo, nigga, you thought this was over?"

Dollar opened his eyes. "What the fuck?"

"Yea, nigga, Hittman Boyz."

All you heard were gunshots as they shot Dollar up in the bed. His body fell on the floor. They shot him two more times before disappearing out of the room, leaving him in a pool of blood.

Chapter 34

"Pay me my money. Matter fact, fuck that. Pay me in bud."

Shady was talking shit as he rolled dice in the lobby of Diane Projects when Cordial stalked up on him.

"You down here rolling dice when you need to be upstairs counting that money."

"I am counting money. I'm down here counting these niggas' money as I break their pockets."

"Shady, you need to tighten up."

"Cordial, all we do is count money and bag up dope. I'm just down here smoking a blunt and fucking with the homie."

"You know how Malachi is."

"Malachi, ain't here. That nigga shut the farm down and went ghost on us. He left us in the jungle with the lions, tigers, and bears."

"He has his reasons why he did what he did."

"Yo, I don't need the *I Have a Dream* speech. I'm on my way up there now."

"We need to talk when you get up there too."

"Copy that, man."

Cordial knew how Shady felt. Everybody felt some type of way about Malachi bouncing, but sometimes you had to stop the first Domino from falling. In Malachi's heart, that was him and Cordial knew that.

***

"Where was his body found?" Nicki asked as she looked down at Dollar's dead body under a white sheet.

"His body was behind a dumpster over there on 127th behind the burger spot." Wild-B said.

"He's naked. That means he was setup by a bitch. We find her, we find the walking dead."

Drama regarded Nicki. "I don't know the bitch's name, but I know how she looks. He told me he was going over on the east side of Harlem to see the bitch."

"Mayham and Drama, bring me this bitch alive. Wild-B, take Dollar's body to AJ Funeral Home. Don't worry about the police report. I'll take care of that. I know someone. Remember dead or alive, we take care of our own."

"When we get her, where you want us to bring her?"

"The auto part garage. I want the bitch to feel a pain like never before. Look at my ape laying there. That bitch is going to lay on that same board, but I won't hear her cries or see her tears. Y'all are my gorillaz. Go beat on your chest and show them who the fuck run Harlem because whoever did this put a gun to their heads and committed suicide."

***

Jasmine walked around her office in an all-black designer dress. Her hair was pulled to the back in a ponytail. She had a diamond chain around her neck and matching earrings on. She was wearing all-black open toe red bottom two inch shoes. Mr. Rice couldn't take his eyes off of her as she was coming from the bar with glasses of Moet. She smiled as she passed him a glass.

"Thank you, Jasmine."

Jasmine sat across from him at the table.

"You are welcome."

Jasmine took a sip then placed her glass down on the table.

"So, this is your word without a doubt that you can make good on 20 kilos a month?"

"This is *my guarantee*, and my product is 100% pure, no cut, and all deliveries will be on time."

"How much per kilo?"

"I can do $24,000 each one. You can cut it up three times and you will still have a strong drug."

"Can I see that sample now?"

"Sure," Jasmine picked the bag up that was on the side of the table and placed a kilo of cocaine on the table in front of Mr. Rice. He pulled out a clear glass vessel with a liquid in it. He cut a small hole on the top of the kilo and took some of the cocaine and placed some of it in the vessel. He watched it for a few seconds and then the liquid turned blue. He did this two more times.

"Like I said Mr. Rice, 100% pure cocaine."

"Jasmine, you stand on your word behind your product. I will have the money wired over to you for 20 kilos today."

"And the location you want your shipment?"

"I will send all the information with the wire transfer."

"That works for me."

Jasmine got up and shook Mr. Rice's hand before he exited out of the door.

Chapter 35

"You see this bitch sitting down laughing and joking like shit is sweet, Mayham?"

"Yeah, who them bitches she with?"

"I don't fucking know, but this shit got me blown. Out here like she the untouchable, like we ain't talking about shit."

"Yo, check it out. Ain't that the nigga J- Right that just pulled up in the drop top Benz?"

"Yeah, that's that nigga J-Right. He popping his shit, thinking he getting a little bite of B-Luv."

"Word is he fuck with them Hittman Boyz. They say he put them on and look who is getting out the car with that nigga."

"I see Beckey with the good hair."

"So, what you thinking?"

"Nigga, you already know what it is, two birds one stone."

"Yo. I'ma yoke Beckey up with the good hair. You roll that nigga in the wipe."

"Fucking right. Let's do this."

Drama and Mayham put their murder one mask over their faces as they watched Beckey with the good hair get in the droptop Benz. When the Benz stopped at the light, Drama pulled the black Explorer in front of the car and jumped out running to the side of the car, shooting J-Right five times in the chest. Mayham snatched Beckey up by her hair and dragged her out by her hair to the back of the Ford Explorer, putting a gun to her face.

"Bitch, you must've thought this shit was sweet like cotton candy. News flash you just been erased."

Drama pulled off the scene, leaving J-Right dead at the red light.

***

"Don't you think it's a little too early in the day to be having a drink?"

Captain Fuller looked at Agent Dawn as he sat down at the bar next to him.

"How's you know I was here?"

"I'm an FBI agent. It's my job to know things, Fuller."

"So, what brings you down here, Dawn?"

"The killing in Harlem. I thought I'd let you know."

"I'm at the point where I don't even give a fuck about shit no more. You see a dead body. You see a million."

"I think the correct way that go is, 'you seen one, you seen a thousand,' not a million, Fuller."

"You know what the fuck I meant, smart ass."

"Yeah. They got a Tracy Banks, street name J-Right, killed early today, shot five times at the red light."

"What's your thought on that, Dawn?"

"Stacy Hall, aka, Nicki Guns."

"Dawn, why the hell do we even try? We had Malachi dead to the wrong star witness, and he still beat us. The fact is they are too rich. Their money is too powerful, and from the police report I read when he had Mike Powell, one of Malachi's own crew members hit him three times in the chest, killing him so we wouldn't get to him. I guess they don't want to make the same mistake again. So, the bad guy killed the bad guy, so the good guy doesn't get the bad guy. Dawn, they are killing their own."

"Fuller, if we give up, the world would be full of bad guys. There are still a lot of good people out there that need us, that still believe in us."

"So, you want to take a trip to Harlem?"

"I thought you would never ask."

"You driving?"

"I don't mind. I don't mind."

***

"Nicki's on her way here now. I just got off the phone with her."

"Sayless, Nicki is cold-blooded with a black heart. She ripped two niggas apart just for talking about licking us, and this bitch set one of her gorrillaz up to get bodied. Yo, Mayham, I know she got all types of evil shit she thinking about right now."

"Real talk. I'm glad my ass not on that table. I really don't even want to see this shit."

"Well, my guy, you ain't want to see this shit. It's too late now. The garage door just opened and the Maybach is pulling in."

Mayham and Drama watched as Cali opened the back door for Nicki to get out. That's when they saw the two pit-bulls come out the car then Nicki gliding their way. She pulled her Prada glasses off and questioned the both of them.

"Where'd you get her at?"

Drama smiled.

"We caught them at the red light."

"Them? I only see her."

"Yeah, them bullets took son's breath away. He couldn't make this trip. Matter of fact, he ain't going to be making no more trips—facts."

"That's my gorilla, go ahead and beat on your chest."

Nicki walked past both of them and right up to Beckey, scowling down at her.

"So, you set Dollar up to be killed then you walked around Harlem like my gorillaz wasn't going to find you in the jungle?"

Beckey started crying while looking at Nicki. Nicki said in a low tone, "I don't see your tears. I don't hear your cries. Strip this bitch down to nothing, Drama and Mayham."

Nicki watched as they beat her and ripped her clothes off until she was naked and in a ball on the floor.

"Pebbles and Bam Bam, come here, babies."

Both pit-bulls ran next to Nicki and sat down next to her. Still balled up, Beckey spotted them while Drama cut his eyes at Mayham.

"Yo, I think she about to let them pits fuck her over."

"You already know she is."

Nicki commanded both of her dogs.

"Stay. Stay."

She waltzed up to Beckey. "I'ma ask you one time and one time only. I want to know who you set Dollar up for and where are they?"

"It was J-Right and Hit'em Up. They said they were just going to jump on him. They didn't tell me they were going to kill him. I swear, please don't kill me."

Nicki turned around and walked over to Mayham and Drama in the dim-lit auto part garage.

"Do either one of y'all know J-Right or Hit'em Up?"

"Yeah, J-Right was the nigga I flatlined when we grabbed this bitch up." Drama confessed.

"What about Hit'em Up?"

"I ain't seen the nigga, but I know who he is."

"Then you need to find him then, like yesterday. I want that man's body here dead or alive."

"You know we on it."

"Good because I know my gorillaz don't play with it."

"What we going do with her now?"

Nicki looked over her. "Oh yea, Pebbles and Bam Bam… eat."

Beckey yelled as both pit-bulls ran and attacked her, ripping her flesh apart, biting her, and shaking her like she was a rag doll.

***

"They said it was a black SUV Ford. Two masked men jumped out, shot the driver, killed him, then grabbed the female up, putting her inside the SUV after smacking her in the face with the gun."

Captain Fuller inspected the crime scene as Agent Dawn was talking.

"Somebody is out to prove that they are the big bad wolf and if they killed him, kidnapped the girl, she knows something. Somebody wants to talk with her. We need to find that black SUV and the motherfucker who grabbed her before we find her, but not the way we want to."

"So, what you thinking, Fuller?"

"It's time to throw the rule book out. We tried it that way already. We're dealing with street niggas who don't give a fuck about the rules. That's the only way we are going to get them."

Agent Dawn punched fists with Captain Fuller as they got in his car.

Chapter 36

"How did that meeting go with Mr. Rice?" Kareem asked.

"Good, he just ordered 20 kilos."

"That's good because I told him when we have a meeting at the other night clubs, that's business, but when we have a meeting here, that's family. With him shopping with us now, we have all the major night clubs on lock in Brooklyn. We just have to keep moving like we are now and there's no stopping us."

Kareem lit his cigar as he talked to Jasmine.

"How you think Cordial and Shady are doing out in New Jersey?"

"I don't know, but I know they are good. Shady's hungry and Cordial is deadly."

"What about Malachi?"

"I try not to think about him. You know the last thing he said to me one on one?"

"No, tell me."

"Next time I fuck up, he was going to kill me."

"Do you think he was for real?"

"I looked in his eyes and they told me he was going to do what he said he was going to do."

Jasmine stepped right up to Kareem's face.

"Well, he's not here now and you are the captain of this ship now."

Kareem lowered his head and kissed Jasmine after she said that.

***

"Y'all need to look around, bodies are dropping... 6 of the homies got laid out on our block. J-Right just got clapped at the red light. They done kidnapped Beckey. All this is going down because two whack ass niggas pulled up talking about kicking these gorillaz or apes, whatever the fuck they call themselves, and now, we are at fucking war."

"Kidd, that was all J-Right and Hit'em Up. J-Right ain't like that shit from the jump. When he found out they were over there eating, J-Right, Hit'em Up, and Beckey did that shit. Those three were talking about the lick, no one else."

"Where is Hit'em Up at now?"

"That nigga went MIA when he found out that J-Right got clapped and Beckey got grabbed."

"So, this nigga is *the one* who talked about the lick to these off brand niggas, got the homies bodied, set Dollar up to get killed, shit went zero to hundred, and this nigga picked up his bags and bounced, leaving niggas in the storm?"

"You just said it play by play."

Kidd looked at Sid and pointed at him.

"You know what? Fuck Hit'em Up. I think I know how we all could win, end this fucking war we are losing, and get a new plug."

Everyone heeded Kidd's words.

"Shit, you have our attention. What's the move?" Sid checked.

"Let me reach out to someone first. Y'all just be on point till I get back."

Kidd turned around and left.

Chapter 37

Shady was smoking a blunt and bopping his head to Lil Baby when Cordial walked up to him. Shady cut his eyes at him, then passed him the blunt.

"Shady, right now, we are all I have. I already know you are 38 hot with Malachi, but Malachi is loyal to us. His loyalty came with the price of leaving us so what we built up, don't fall down. The feds had one man in their eye and that was *him*. Real talk, Nicki dropped a haymaker on him at the meeting. If one of us got locked up, we are looking at the death sentence just because we are associated with Malachi. They can hit us with association by following the money trail, association by organizing crime, association by murder, yet we all eating still. Don't take him bouncing on us as a sign of disloyalty. Take it as a sign of loyalty because what he did was to protect us."

"I was on my bag about that, but you just said some real shit. I was just thinking about shit from my point of view."

"I already know, baby boy."

Shady dapped Cordial up.

"On another note, come on. We need to go make a brick run. We only have three left."

"Fuck it. We out."

Cordial patted Shady on the back as they walked out the spot.

***

Nicki's Maybach pulled up two blocks over from Rukus Park in a back alley. Drama, Mayham, and Wild-B were standing next to Kidd and Sid beside Kidd's car with their guns drawn as they waited for her to step out the car. Kidd had never seen Nicki. He didn't know who she was in the car. He looked at Sid as the driver of the Maybach got out of the car in a suit and walked around to the back door, opening it.

That's when he saw Nicki step out. They couldn't believe how beautiful she was. She was bossed up all the way. Kidd and Sid knew gorrilaz and apes were in Harlem now. She walked up to them and took her Prada glasses off. She eyed Drama, Mayham, and Wild-B and then them.

"You asked to see the boss, so they called *me*. Who are you?"

"My name is Kidd and I don't know what you heard about us trying to rob you or set you up. We had nothing to do with that."

Nicki pointed her finger at both of them before talking. "Y'all are the Hittem Boyz who killed my ape? Drama, why are they still alive?"

Mayhem and Wild-B stepped forward an put their guns to Kidd and Sid's heads when she said that.

"Wait, wait... just hear what I have to say first."

Nicki put her hand up and motioned for them to put their guns down. "Talk."

"On God, we ain't had shit to do with that. The nigga behind all that shit, we have him for you right now."

"You have him right now for me?"

"Buddy in the trunk right now... gift wrapped and all."

"Mayham and Wild-B, move them two to the dumpster right there. Drama, open the trunk."

Drama moved to the trunk and opened it, looking inside at a duct taped Hit'em Up, then veered back at Nicki.

"Son, this right here's like a package under the tree wrapped up."

"Pull him out."

Drama pulled Hit'em Up out of the trunk, prompting Hit'em Up to shift his eyes to Nicki. His eyes became big as dollar coins.

"Kill him and throw his body in the dumpster."

Putting the gun to his head, Drama pulled the trigger, killing Hit'em Up. Then Mayham helped Drama throw his body into the dumpster. Nicki deflected to Kidd and Sid.

"What y'all two did was disloyalty. You brought a rabbit to a wolf."

"No, what *he* did was disloyalty by putting us in all this bullshit and then hiding."

"You make a good point."

"Can we stop walking on eggshells now?"

"Stay in your lane. The first time you step out of it, that genie ain't going back in that bottle. We are good. I have no problem with you."

Nicki looked at Drama and winked at him before going back to her car.

"Drama, the deal was that I bring you this nigga, the beef is dead, and you will supply for us now. She ain't say nothing about that."

Drama viewed Kidd.

"She did. You just didn't see her. You good. Whatever you need, we got."

Chapter 38

Malachi was sitting on the deck smoking a cigar with two stress balls in his hands in deep thought when Mrs. Blanka opened the deck doors and stepped outside, sitting next to Malachi. She rested her hand on his lap and Malachi turned to her.

"I see you are deep in thought. Do you want to talk about it?"

"You were right. She's stronger than everybody. She moves different, act different, thinks different, and she didn't even second guess to kill B-More."

"Malachi, an apex predator will kill their young. They will do everything to survive and protect their territory. Did she say why she killed him?"

"She did. She said she didn't trust him, in not so many words so she killed him before the police could get to him. She called his name then shot him 3 times in the chest, killing him in cold blood."

"She killed him before he could become a traitor. She called his name so he could see her face. She was letting him know it's not personal. It's just business."

"She said that she killed him to protect the cartel and me."

"She was right. You are thinking about her or are you thinking about if you made the right choice by leaving?"

"I am thinking about her. I've been down here with you for the last eight months and I ask myself, how are they moving without me?"

"Won't you go to New York and see. I'll take care of things down here while you are gone."

"Are you sure… because I always had my eyes on her?"

"Yeah, I am. I'll be waiting on you when you get back."

160

Malachi got up and kissed Mrs. Blanka on the cheek before walking off the deck. He stopped when Mrs. Blanka called his name. "Malachi, tell her how you feel and that you have always been watching her."

***

Cali pulled the car over as he looked into the rearview mirror at the cop car that pulled him over.

"Nicki, it's the same cop from the restaurant the other day that just pulled us over."

"You think he would see the big picture, but I see sometimes, you have to show and prove to these motherfuckers who they are dealing with."

Captain Fuller stepped out of the car and walked up to the Maybach, knocking on the back window. Nicki rolled her window down and looked at Captain Fuller.

"May I help you?"

"I'm just trying to see how I can go from driving a Ford to a Maybach with a personal driver. Something like how you went from talking about the cartel to being a part of the Black Diamond Cartel."

"I don't know nothing about what you are talking about, Captain Fuller."

"If you say so. Tell Malachi he can't hide from us even with his new face and different voice. Let him know his day is coming soon."

"Again, I don't know nothing about what you are talking about with this conversation."

"I know you don't… take care, Nicki Guns."

Nicki didn't say a word. She rolled up her car window as Cali pulled off.

"You still think it's too early in the day to be killing cops?"

"I think Captain Fuller could use a real message as a reminder that he's not a superhero and real life cops die."

"What you have in mind?"

"Let's blow up his car and if he tries us again, a lot of officers will have a black band over their badges."

"As you wish."

Nicki's car pulled up in front of the plaza. Cali got out and opened the door for her. She walked through the lobby to the elevator. Once in her penthouse she opened the door and looked around. The penthouse smelled like Cuban cigars. She searched her home but didn't see anybody. She saw both of her dogs looking at her. She walked back out the penthouse to her parked car in the parking garage, got in, and drove off.

Chapter 39

Captain Fuller stepped out of his front door, pressed the alarm for his car to unlock the doors, and that's when his car blew up. He jumped back and just watched his car go up in flames as he bit down on his lip.

***

"I had a strong feeling that you would know to come here."

Malachi never turned around as he talked. When the office door opened Nicki walked inside.

"This is where you been all along?"

Malachi turned around and looked at Nicki.

"No, I've only been back 24 hours."

"Why did you come back?"

"To check on you."

"Do you want me to believe that?"

Malachi walked up to Nicki.

"I have always been in the picture, from all the things you were doing in Harlem with your gorillaz and apes, I have always watched you, Nicki. So yes, I want you to believe that."

"Am I the only one you been watching?"

"No." Malachi went and sat on the desk as he lit his cigar.

"Who else then?"

"Jasmine and Kareem in Brooklyn. They are working with a few of my old connects, taking over night clubs one at a time. Cordial and Shady are still in New Jersey working with what I gave them. You are the only one who made their own way as I did ten years ago before I had the Black Diamond Cartel."

"I did what I had to do to stand on my own. There's no going back to who I used to be… never."

"I know. That's why I'm here because you and I can take over more than just the east coast together. Together, there will be no stopping us."

"Malachi, there are choices we make that make us who we are. I was beat, raped, I killed innocent people, I never questioned what I had to do. I never let my heart get in the way. You made my heart *black*. When I kill, I have no remorse, but you still believe in letting a spark breathe till it turns into a fire. The first time a mistake. The second time is just fucking weak hearted and stupid. Mrs. Blanka thought you were the one that could take her son's place, but you let Cruise live. Who knew she called the hit on Manny and you kidnapped him for her That was a spark that could've been a deadly fire."

"How the fuck do you know all of this?"

"Because we had more than a conversation about trafficking females, Malachi. We talked about how she needed me to do what you couldn't. There aren't no packs between wolves and sheep. It's just an apex predator and prey. Weakness will get you killed."

"Are you calling me *prey*?"

Malachi looked at the door when he heard Mrs. Blanka's voice.

"No, she's not calling you prey. She's calling you *weak*."

Malachi turned around and looked at Nicki and was lost for words when he saw the gun she had pointed at him.

"I killed Cruise and brought Mrs. Blanka his head. I did what you couldn't."

"So, what now, Nicki? I made you. Where do we go from here?"

"You die."

Nicki shot Malachi four times in the chest then she strolled up to him as he was laying on the floor with blood coming out of his mouth and shot him one more time in the head, killing him. Mrs. Blanka joined Nicki and peered down at Malachi's dead body laying in a pool of blood.

"The man who broke you, abused you… you looked into his eyes and killed him today. You know what that means? He was only human."

"So, what now?"

"You take the crown and run things."

Chapter 40

Kareem couldn't believe what he was hearing. Jasmine watched him as he paced the floor.

"Alright. Thank you for the call." Kareem hung up the phone and looked at Jasmine. She knew something was wrong by the look in his eyes.

"That was Mrs. Blanka. She just told me Malachi is dead."

"Don't tell me that, Kareem. Please don't tell me that!"

"I wish I didn't have to. She's having his body sent up here so we can lay him to rest."

"How did he die?"

"Cruise and Manny's cartel, but she said they killed Cruise in a shoot-out."

Jasmine sat down on the couch as a tear came from her eye. She loved Malachi more than any other. She still didn't want to believe the truth. She was hoping it was a lie.

***

Shady sat on the stairs looking down on the ground as he had both hands on his gun as tears fell on his eyes. Malachi was like a father to him. He thought back to that day when Malachi walked up to him in the park. From that day on, Malachi was the man he wanted to be. Cordial looked out the window at Shady. He knew how he felt. Malachi was his brother who brought him into this game and now the game he showed him how they killed him. Cordial walked to the bar and poured himself a drink.

"Rest in peace, my nigga, I love you."

Cordial thought Malachi would be saying them words to him, but it was going to be him saying them over Malachi.

Cordial wiped the tear drop from his eye as hate filled his heart.

Chapter 41

Nicki walked up to Malachi's casket and placed a red rose down on his chest and kissed his forehead then whispered in his ear, "The night I killed you, it made my pussy wet. You made me an apex predator, a shark. Everything you had done to me, the beatings, the rapes, the killing innocent people you made me kill, the cocaine you made me sell, it didn't break me. You can't drown a shark and if you break down the five letters in shark, it stands for strategic, hunter, aggressive, respected, king. I will forever wear this stamp, the Black Diamond Cartel, but now, it's time for me to start my empire, The Bloodstone Kartel."

Nicki kissed Malachi's cheek then walked out the church to her car where Cali was waiting on her. He opened the door as she got in.

"Take me to my penthouse."

"Yes ma'am."

***

"I don't give a fuck what you think, Kareem. I know she had her hands in Malachi's death, and what the fuck did she whisper in his ear?"

"Jasmine, you don't know that."

"Nigga, open your eyes. She dropped a rose on his fucking chest, whispered in his ear, and walked out the fucking church. She been playing us and I know what the fuck I'ma do."

"Jasmine, think about this."

"I already have."

Kareem watched as Jasmine walked out the brownstone, not even bothering trying to stop her.

***

Nicki stepped out of her car and Captain Fuller stomped up to her.

"I heard a penthouse here is $6,000 a month."

Nicki looked at him and cut her eyes.

"What do you want, Captain Fuller?"

"I really did like that car."

"What's your point?"

"I could have been killed."

"It's still not too late, captain. If you ever show up here again, it will be more than your car that blows up next time."

"Are you sure you want to play this game, Nicki?"

Nicki strode up to Captain Fuller and looked into his eyes.

"The game already started, captain. The first quarter was when you and Agent Dawn walked into my diner. The second quarter was when you pulled my car over. The third quarter was your car blowing up. This is the fourth quarter and if we have to go into overtime, let's just say King James couldn't keep my team off your ass. When it's go time, walk off, captain. Let's not do overtime."

"Nicki, if I get killed behind my badge, what do you think will happen next?"

"Everyone will put a black band over their badge. Then an investigation will follow by a funeral and a burial. In so many words, *fuck your threats*. Captain, tread lightly because you are walking on eggshells."

"Well hey, you can't make an omelet without breaking a few eggs. Hey Nicki, I'll catch you soon."

Nicki smiled and walked inside the plaza.

Chapter 42

"You left me, dog. Like fuck, man. How they catch you down bad? Shit ain't even the same no more. Jasmine and Kareem are doing their own thing. Cordial ain't even the same no more. We broke the bricks down the middle, and I had to put my back on him. Ain't nobody heard from Nicki, but word is she got a group of gorillaz that're killers and beating on their chests, fucking up Harlem. As for me, I'm just going back to wait. I know without you, it's just rainy days and fucked up nights. The Black Diamond Cartel were family. We don't kick it, laugh, or joke no more. It's like when we see each other, it's hi and bye, but when you stamped us, it was do or die. Look, I brought you something."

Shady pulled out a chess piece and laid it down next to Malachi's headstone. That's when Nicki's car pulled up to the graveyard a few feet back from Malachi's resting spot. She looked out her window at Shady standing next to his headstone. She opened the door and walked over to him, but she stopped walking when she heard him talking. She waited until he stopped talking to call his name.

"Shady."

Shady turned around and looked at Nicki then at Cali standing next to her Maybach.

"I heard you were in Harlem, turning the streets into a blood bath, leaving a body count to make a point."

"Sometimes killing is the only language motherfuckers understand. That's something Malachi made me understand."

"He made me understand that too."

"I see you are paying your respects to Malachi."

"First, I'm going to lay these roses down on Malachi's grave then I'm going to Harlem and if you want, you can come with me. Malachi is dead, but the Black Diamond Cartel still lives. We are proof of that."

Nicki walked past Shady and laid the roses down next to Malachi's headstone then kissed two of her fingers and placed them down on the headstone. Then she walked back to Shady.

"So where do you go from here, Shady?"

"I guess with you. Cordial is back on his Billy the Kid shit. Jasmine and Kareem are acting like Jay-Z and Beyonce, so what's in Harlem for me?"

"A new start, a new beginning."

Shady nodded as Nicki walked up to him and grabbed his hand, leading him to her Maybach. Cali opened the door for them.

"Shady, where can I find Cordial? I need you to take me to him."

Shady nodded.

***

"What the fuck I tell y'all about rolling dice in this hallway? Y'all niggas must think I'm pussy or a joke?"

"Cordial, you tripping… niggas ain't taking you as no joke or thinking you're a pussy, but we been in this hallway way before you pulled up on this block claiming this building. My guy, you need to understand and trust and believe we ain't pussy. We respect you, but our hearts pump the same blood yours do."

Cordial sucked his teeth and nodded.

"You know what, little nigga? Y'all's hearts do pump the same blood as mine does, but I'm at a point where I don't give a fuck. My nigga just got bodied. I'ma show y'all niggas my bite is harder than my bark."

Cordial pulled his gun out and shot both of them in the chest. Walking over to them, he pointed his gun at their heads and shot them in the face, point blank range.

"The difference between me and your hearts is my shit is still pumping blood, motherfucker."

Nicki and Shady walked in the building and regarded Cordial as he held his gun in his hand. Nicki slowly walked up to both bodies and peered down at them as Cordial looked at her. She turned around and studied Cordial.

"So what are you going to do with the bodies now?"

Cordial didn't say nothing. He looked at Shady then Nicki. Shady nodded at him.

"I don't know."

"You have any work here?"

"No"

"Then fuck it then. Let's get out of here."

Chapter 43

Jasmine stepped out of her car in Harlem and eased up to Cali. She been watching him for the last few days. Cali smiled when he spotted Jasmine walking his way.

"Jasmine, it's been forever since I seen you. What brings you to Harlem?"

"I just go where the wind blows. I ain't see you at Malachi's funeral. Why is that?"

"I was there. I just didn't go inside. I didn't want to see him laying in a casket like that."

Nicki walked to the auto part shop window and spotted Jasmine talking to Cali.

"You know, Cali, I remember when Malachi opened the doors for you to come into this family."

"I do too."

"I heard about the things Nicki been doing out here. She took Harlem overnight, you can say."

"Jasmine, I know you. I know you are a killer and you are loyal to Malachi. I know you are in Harlem for a reason so don't bullshit me. What's the real reason you are out here?"

Jasmine stood next to Cali and whispered in his ear. "I know and you know that there is more to Malachi's murder than what we are being told. I just hope what we were told was the truth because if not, a lot more motherfuckers are going to die."

"Why are you telling me this?"

"Because if I find out you had a part in his death, the last suit you will be wearing would be in a wooden box. *If* I decide I want them to find your body. Now do me a favor and be a good boy and tell Nicki Guns I said *hi*. Would you do that for me?"

Jasmine smiled and turned, walking back to her car. She got in and drove off. Cali watched her leave. Once Nicki saw her leave, she walked back to the back of the auto part shop in deep thought.

***

Captain Fuller sat at his desk when Chief Ward walked into his office.

"I never seen that look on your face before, Fuller."

"What look is that, Chief?"

"Like the dog fight is out of you."

"Chief, we are fighting a battle that we can't win. Our backs been against the ropes the whole fight."

"Yeah, you're right, but just because your back is against the ropes don't mean we can't win."

"Let's look at the big picture here. They are too powerful. They are too rich. They money is too tempting."

"So, what does that mean, we can't win? Let me school you on something, Fuller. Nobody wins when they go toe to toe with the great law enforcement force in the world, The NYPD! When they shoot, we shoot. When they kill, we kill. We took an oath to protect the law so if you have to bend the law to get the bad guys off the streets, bend them and let me take care of the rest. This fight ain't over. It just started."

"Bend the rules, Chief?"

"Yeah, and off record, if you have to break them, then break them motherfuckers."

"Say no more, Chief."

Chief Ward left Captain Fuller's office. Captain Fuller picked up the phone and made a call. After a few seconds someone picked up.

"It's Fuller. Get ready. We are to shake the streets, old school way."

After saying that he hung up the phone.

Chapter 44

Nicki moseyed into her penthouse and focused on her picture on the wall of the globe of the world with the words around it. It said, *the world is yours.* Reaching into her pocket and pulling out a cigar, for the first time in her life, she lit the cigar and puffed it. She looked back at the picture and declared, "I know the world is mine," as both of her dogs ran up to her, jumping on her as her eyes remained locked on the picture on her wall.

"And the rest of the world is about to learn that lesson as well…just you wait and see."

TO BE CONTINUED…

Lock Down Publications and Ca$h Presents
Assisted Publishing Packages

BASIC PACKAGE	UPGRADED PACKAGE
$499	$800
Editing	Typing
Cover Design	Editing
Formatting	Cover Design
	Formatting
ADVANCE PACKAGE	**LDP SUPREME PACKAGE**
$1,200	$1,500
Typing	Typing
Editing	Editing
Cover Design	Cover Design
Formatting	Formatting
Copyright registration	Copyright registration
Proofreading	Proofreading
Upload book to Amazon	Set up Amazon account
	Upload book to Amazon
	Advertise on LDP, Amazon and Facebook Page

Other services available upon request.
Additional charges may apply
Lock Down Publications
P.O. Box 944
Stockbridge, GA 30281-9998
Phone: 470 303-9761

Submission Guideline

Submit the first three chapters of your completed manuscript to ldpsubmissions@gmail.com, subject line: Your book's title. The manuscript must be in a .doc file and sent as an attachment. Document should be in Times New Roman, double spaced and in size 12 font. Also, provide your synopsis and full contact information. If sending multiple submissions, they must each be in a separate email.

Have a story but no way to send it electronically? You can still submit to LDP/Ca$h Presents. Send in the first three chapters, written or typed, of your completed manuscript to:

LDP: Submissions Dept
Po Box 944
Stockbridge, Ga 30281

DO NOT send original manuscript. Must be a duplicate.

Provide your synopsis and a cover letter containing your full contact information.

Thanks for considering LDP and Ca$h Presents.

NEW RELEASES

SOSA GANG 2 by ROMELL TUKES
KINGZ OF THE GAME 7 by PLAYA RAY
SKI MASK MONEY 2 by RENTA
BORN IN THE GRAVE 3 by SELF MADE TAY
LOYALTY IS EVERYTHING 3 by MOLOTTI

Coming Soon from Lock Down Publications/Ca$h Presents

BLOOD OF A BOSS **VI**
SHADOWS OF THE GAME II
TRAP BASTARD II
By Askari
LOYAL TO THE GAME **IV**
By T.J. & Jelissa
TRUE SAVAGE **VIII**
MIDNIGHT CARTEL IV
DOPE BOY MAGIC IV
CITY OF KINGZ III
NIGHTMARE ON SILENT AVE II
THE PLUG OF LIL MEXICO II
CLASSIC CITY II
By Chris Green
BLAST FOR ME **III**
A SAVAGE DOPEBOY III
CUTTHROAT MAFIA III
DUFFLE BAG CARTEL VII
HEARTLESS GOON VI
By Ghost
A HUSTLER'S DECEIT III
KILL ZONE II
BAE BELONGS TO ME III
TIL DEATH II
By Aryanna
KING OF THE TRAP III
By T.J. Edwards
GORILLAZ IN THE BAY V
3X KRAZY III
STRAIGHT BEAST MODE III

De'Kari
KINGPIN KILLAZ IV
STREET KINGS III
PAID IN BLOOD III
CARTEL KILLAZ IV
DOPE GODS III
Hood Rich
SINS OF A HUSTLA II
ASAD
YAYO V
Bred In The Game 2
S. Allen
THE STREETS WILL TALK II
By Yolanda Moore
SON OF A DOPE FIEND III
HEAVEN GOT A GHETTO III
SKI MASK MONEY III
By Renta
LOYALTY AIN'T PROMISED III
By Keith Williams
I'M NOTHING WITHOUT HIS LOVE II
SINS OF A THUG II
TO THE THUG I LOVED BEFORE II
IN A HUSTLER I TRUST II
By Monet Dragun
QUIET MONEY IV
EXTENDED CLIP III
THUG LIFE IV
By Trai'Quan
THE STREETS MADE ME IV
By Larry D. Wright
IF YOU CROSS ME ONCE III
ANGEL V
By Anthony Fields

THE STREETS WILL NEVER CLOSE IV
By K'ajji
HARD AND RUTHLESS III
KILLA KOUNTY IV
By Khufu
MONEY GAME III
By Smoove Dolla
JACK BOYS VS DOPE BOYS IV
A GANGSTA'S QUR'AN V
COKE GIRLZ II
COKE BOYS II
LIFE OF A SAVAGE V
CHI'RAQ GANGSTAS V
SOSA GANG III
BRONX SAVAGES II
BODYMORE KINGPINS II
By Romell Tukes
MURDA WAS THE CASE III
Elijah R. Freeman
AN UNFORESEEN LOVE IV
BABY, I'M WINTERTIME COLD III
By Meesha

QUEEN OF THE ZOO III
By Black Migo
CONFESSIONS OF A JACKBOY III
By Nicholas Lock
KING KILLA II
By Vincent "Vitto" Holloway
BETRAYAL OF A THUG III
By Fre$h
THE MURDER QUEENS III
By Michael Gallon
THE BIRTH OF A GANGSTER III
By Delmont Player
TREAL LOVE II

By Le'Monica Jackson
FOR THE LOVE OF BLOOD III
By Jamel Mitchell
RAN OFF ON DA PLUG II
By Paper Boi Rari
HOOD CONSIGLIERE III
By Keese
PRETTY GIRLS DO NASTY THINGS II
By Nicole Goosby
PROTÉGÉ OF A LEGEND III
LOVE IN THE TRENCHES II
By Corey Robinson
IT'S JUST ME AND YOU II
By Ah'Million
FOREVER GANGSTA III
By Adrian Dulan
GORILLAZ IN THE TRENCHES II
By SayNoMore
THE COCAINE PRINCESS VIII
By King Rio
CRIME BOSS II
Playa Ray
LOYALTY IS EVERYTHING III
Molotti
HERE TODAY GONE TOMORROW II
By Fly Rock
REAL G'S MOVE IN SILENCE II
By Von Diesel
GRIMEY WAYS IV
By Ray Vinci

Available Now

RESTRAINING ORDER **I & II**
By CA$H & Coffee
LOVE KNOWS NO BOUNDARIES **I II & III**
By Coffee
RAISED AS A GOON I, II, III & IV
BRED BY THE SLUMS I, II, III
BLAST FOR ME I & II
ROTTEN TO THE CORE I II III
A BRONX TALE I, II, III
DUFFLE BAG CARTEL I II III IV V VI
HEARTLESS GOON I II III IV V
A SAVAGE DOPEBOY I II
DRUG LORDS I II III
CUTTHROAT MAFIA I II
KING OF THE TRENCHES
By Ghost
LAY IT DOWN **I & II**
LAST OF A DYING BREED I II
BLOOD STAINS OF A SHOTTA I & II III
By Jamaica
LOYAL TO THE GAME I II III
LIFE OF SIN I, II III
By TJ & Jelissa
BLOODY COMMAS I & II
SKI MASK CARTEL I II & III
KING OF NEW YORK I II,III IV V
RISE TO POWER I II III
COKE KINGS I II III IV V
BORN HEARTLESS I II III IV
KING OF THE TRAP I II
By T.J. Edwards
IF LOVING HIM IS WRONG…I & II

LOVE ME EVEN WHEN IT HURTS I II III
By Jelissa
WHEN THE STREETS CLAP BACK I & II III
THE HEART OF A SAVAGE I II III IV
MONEY MAFIA I II
LOYAL TO THE SOIL I II III
By Jibril Williams
A DISTINGUISHED THUG STOLE MY HEART I II
& III
LOVE SHOULDN'T HURT I II III IV
RENEGADE BOYS I II III IV
PAID IN KARMA I II III
SAVAGE STORMS I II III
AN UNFORESEEN LOVE I II III
BABY, I'M WINTERTIME COLD I II
By Meesha
A GANGSTER'S CODE I &, II III
A GANGSTER'S SYN I II III
THE SAVAGE LIFE I II III
CHAINED TO THE STREETS I II III
BLOOD ON THE MONEY I II III
A GANGSTA'S PAIN I II III
By J-Blunt
PUSH IT TO THE LIMIT
By Bre' Hayes
BLOOD OF A BOSS I, II, III, IV, V
SHADOWS OF THE GAME
TRAP BASTARD
By Askari
THE STREETS BLEED MURDER **I, II & III**
THE HEART OF A GANGSTA I II& III
By Jerry Jackson
CUM FOR ME I II III IV V VI VII VIII
An LDP Erotica Collaboration

BRIDE OF A HUSTLA **I II & II**
THE FETTI GIRLS **I, II& III**
CORRUPTED BY A GANGSTA I, II III, IV
BLINDED BY HIS LOVE
THE PRICE YOU PAY FOR LOVE I, II ,III
DOPE GIRL MAGIC I II III
By Destiny Skai
WHEN A GOOD GIRL GOES BAD
By Adrienne
THE COST OF LOYALTY I II III
By Kweli
A GANGSTER'S REVENGE **I II III & IV**
THE BOSS MAN'S DAUGHTERS I II III IV V
A SAVAGE LOVE **I & II**
BAE BELONGS TO ME I II
A HUSTLER'S DECEIT I, II, III
WHAT BAD BITCHES DO I, II, III
SOUL OF A MONSTER I II III
KILL ZONE
A DOPE BOY'S QUEEN I II III
TIL DEATH
By Aryanna
A KINGPIN'S AMBITON
A KINGPIN'S AMBITION **II**
I MURDER FOR THE DOUGH
By Ambitious
TRUE SAVAGE I II III IV V VI VII
DOPE BOY MAGIC I, II, III
MIDNIGHT CARTEL I II III
CITY OF KINGZ I II
NIGHTMARE ON SILENT AVE
THE PLUG OF LIL MEXICO II
CLASSIC CITY
By Chris Green
A DOPEBOY'S PRAYER
By Eddie "Wolf" Lee

THE KING CARTEL **I, II & III**
By Frank Gresham
THESE NIGGAS AIN'T LOYAL **I, II & III**
By Nikki Tee
GANGSTA SHYT **I II &III**
By CATO
THE ULTIMATE BETRAYAL
By Phoenix
Boss'n Up i , ii & IIi
By Royal Nicole
I LOVE YOU TO DEATH
By Destiny J
I RIDE FOR MY HITTA
I STILL RIDE FOR MY HITTA
By Misty Holt
LOVE & CHASIN' PAPER
By Qay Crockett
TO DIE IN VAIN
SINS OF A HUSTLA
By ASAD
BROOKLYN HUSTLAZ
By Boogsy Morina
BROOKLYN ON LOCK I & II
By Sonovia
GANGSTA CITY
By Teddy Duke
A DRUG KING AND HIS DIAMOND I & II III
A DOPEMAN'S RICHES
HER MAN, MINE'S TOO I, II
CASH MONEY HO'S
THE WIFEY I USED TO BE I II
PRETTY GIRLS DO NASTY THINGS
By Nicole Goosby
TRAPHOUSE KING **I II & III**

KINGPIN KILLAZ I II III
STREET KINGS I II
PAID IN BLOOD **I II**
CARTEL KILLAZ I II III
DOPE GODS I II
By Hood Rich
LIPSTICK KILLAH **I, II, III**
CRIME OF PASSION I II & III
FRIEND OR FOE I II III
By Mimi
STEADY MOBBN' **I, II, III**
THE STREETS STAINED MY SOUL I II III
By Marcellus Allen
WHO SHOT YA **I, II, III**
SON OF A DOPE FIEND I II
HEAVEN GOT A GHETTO I II
SKI MASK MONEY I II
Renta
GORILLAZ IN THE BAY **I II III IV**
TEARS OF A GANGSTA I II
3X KRAZY I II
STRAIGHT BEAST MODE I II
DE'KARI
TRIGGADALE I II III
MURDAROBER WAS THE CASE I II
Elijah R. Freeman
GOD BLESS THE TRAPPERS I, II, III
THESE SCANDALOUS STREETS I, II, III
FEAR MY GANGSTA I, II, III IV, V
THESE STREETS DON'T LOVE NOBODY I, II
BURY ME A G I, II, III, IV, V
A GANGSTA'S EMPIRE I, II, III, IV
THE DOPEMAN'S BODYGAURD I II
THE REALEST KILLAZ I II III
THE LAST OF THE OGS I II III
Tranay Adams

THE STREETS ARE CALLING
Duquie Wilson
MARRIED TO A BOSS I II III
By Destiny Skai & Chris Green
KINGZ OF THE GAME I II III IV V VI VII
CRIME BOSS
Playa Ray
SLAUGHTER GANG I II III
RUTHLESS HEART I II III
By Willie Slaughter
FUK SHYT
By Blakk Diamond
DON'T F#CK WITH MY HEART I II
By Linnea
ADDICTED TO THE DRAMA I II III
IN THE ARM OF HIS BOSS II
By Jamila
YAYO I II III IV
A SHOOTER'S AMBITION I II
BRED IN THE GAME
By S. Allen
TRAP GOD I II III
RICH $AVAGE I II III
MONEY IN THE GRAVE I II III
By Martell Troublesome Bolden
FOREVER GANGSTA I II
 GLOCKS ON SATIN SHEETS I II
By Adrian Dulan
TOE TAGZ I II III IV
LEVELS TO THIS SHYT I II
IT'S JUST ME AND YOU
By Ah'Million
KINGPIN DREAMS I II III
RAN OFF ON DA PLUG

A GANGSTA'S PARADISE
By Trai'Quan
THE STREETS MADE ME I II III
By Larry D. Wright
THE ULTIMATE SACRIFICE I, II, III, IV, V, VI
KHADIFI
IF YOU CROSS ME ONCE I II
ANGEL I II III IV
IN THE BLINK OF AN EYE
By Anthony Fields
THE LIFE OF A HOOD STAR
By Ca$h & Rashia Wilson
THE STREETS WILL NEVER CLOSE I II III
By K'ajji
CREAM I II III
THE STREETS WILL TALK
By Yolanda Moore
NIGHTMARES OF A HUSTLA I II III
By King Dream
CONCRETE KILLA I II III
VICIOUS LOYALTY I II III
By Kingpen
HARD AND RUTHLESS I II
MOB TOWN 251
THE BILLIONAIRE BENTLEYS I II III
REAL G'S MOVE IN SILENCE
By Von Diesel
GHOST MOB
Stilloan Robinson
MOB TIES I II III IV V VI
SOUL OF A HUSTLER, HEART OF A KILLER I II
GORILLAZ IN THE TRENCHES
By SayNoMore
BODYMORE MURDERLAND I II III

THE BIRTH OF A GANGSTER I II
By Delmont Player
FOR THE LOVE OF A BOSS
By C. D. Blue
MOBBED UP I II III IV
THE BRICK MAN I II III IV V
THE COCAINE PRINCESS I II III IV V VI VII
By King Rio
KILLA KOUNTY I II III IV
By Khufu
MONEY GAME I II
By Smoove Dolla
A GANGSTA'S KARMA I II III
By FLAME
KING OF THE TRENCHES I II III
by GHOST & TRANAY ADAMS
QUEEN OF THE ZOO I II
By Black Migo
GRIMEY WAYS I II III
By Ray Vinci
XMAS WITH AN ATL SHOOTER
By Ca$h & Destiny Skai
KING KILLA
By Vincent "Vitto" Holloway
BETRAYAL OF A THUG I II
By Fre$h
THE MURDER QUEENS I II
By Michael Gallon
TREAL LOVE
By Le'Monica Jackson
FOR THE LOVE OF BLOOD I II
By Jamel Mitchell
HOOD CONSIGLIERE I II
By Keese
PROTÉGÉ OF A LEGEND I II
LOVE IN THE TRENCHES

By Corey Robinson
BORN IN THE GRAVE I II III
By Self Made Tay
MOAN IN MY MOUTH
By XTASY
TORN BETWEEN A GANGSTER AND A
GENTLEMAN
By J-BLUNT & Miss Kim
LOYALTY IS EVERYTHING I II
Molotti
HERE TODAY GONE TOMORROW
By Fly Rock
PILLOW PRINCESS
By S. Hawkins

BOOKS BY LDP'S CEO, CA$H